CANAL OF DEATH

A CRIME THRILLER

CHIEF INSPECTOR HOLT
BOOK TWO

NIC SAINT

CANAL OF DEATH

Chief Inspector Holt Book 2

Copyright © 2024 by Nic Saint

Edited by Chereese Graves

www.nicsaint.com

Give feedback on the book at: info@nicsaint.com

facebook.com/nicsaintauthor
@nicsaintauthor

First Edition

Printed in the U.S.A

CANAL OF DEATH

When darkness descends on Ghent, Chief Inspector Holt is drawn into his most chilling case yet.

What begins as a desperate search for a kidnapped plastic surgeon takes a sinister turn when the mutilated body of a woman is discovered in one of the city's canals. The evidence is fragmented, the motives unclear—but one question looms large: are the two cases connected?

As Holt races to untangle the threads, his team is thrown into chaos. A brutal attack on one of their own leads them to secretly pursue a shadowy trail, defying orders and risking everything.

But as the investigation spirals, the stakes grow deadly— and the killer's sights shift dangerously close to Holt's personal world. Betrayal, obsession, and violence collide in a nerve-shredding race against time.

For Holt, this isn't just a case. It's a battle for survival. And in Ghent's darkest corners, no one is safe.

CHAPTER 1

*S*andy McMinn was late. Not that it was his fault. Traffic around Ghent South was terrible as usual, with cars stuck as far as the eye could see—which wasn't far, given that nature had decided to make matters worse by subjecting the harried rush-hour drivers to a steady drizzle that limited visibility and shrouded the entire downtown area in obscurity.

Behind him, Tommy stirred. Unlike his dad, the little tyke was oblivious to the stress that came with supporting both a family and a high-pressure job as one of the country's most sought-after plastic surgeons. And today, of all days, Sandy had an important patient coming in—a member of the royal family, no less, who wasn't entirely happy with her appearance. She had selected Sandy as the go-to person to fix what nature had, in her opinion, failed to deliver.

From the media images the royal palace liked to release from time to time, she appeared to be a perfectly proportioned young woman, not to mention strikingly beautiful in every way. But even the most gorgeous people often find fault with some aspect of their physique—an insecurity they only feel comfortable sharing with a medical professional. If he were a betting man, Sandy would have wagered it was about her breasts. Breast augmentation was still one of the most popular procedures he and his team performed on a daily basis.

The driver in front of him was signaling to merge into the left lane, even though it was clear to anyone that there was no chance he'd be able to join the flow of traffic. All he was doing was stalling his own lane even further.

Sandy resisted the powerful urge to slam on his car horn. He wasn't a violent man, so he suppressed the temptation. Instead, he turned up the volume on his car stereo. The news had come on, and the newscaster was issuing a stern warning: a gang of crooks had been targeting vulnerable elderly people in the small town of Loveringem. These fraudsters had already succeeded in swindling several pensioners out of their hard-earned savings by posing as police officers.

The gall of these people, Sandy thought. Fortunately, his own parents weren't the type to fall for the schemes dreamed up by these lowlifes. Then again, they weren't quite as old as the demographic the newscaster seemed to have in mind.

Sandy switched the radio to a more kid-friendly channel. As a popular song began to play, Tommy perked up and started singing along at the top of his voice.

Sandy grinned and joined in, their voices mingling with the upbeat tune. Moments later, the traffic jam was all but forgotten, and so was the dreadful weather that had held the town of Ghent hostage. Circumstances might have been rough, but having a five-year-old in the car could chase the clouds away and bring out the sunshine.

He was just trying to hit that high note when, all of a sudden, his door was yanked open, and a man wearing a mask pointed a rather large gun directly at his face. As he stared down the barrel of the weapon, the man growled, "Out! Out of the car—now!"

There wasn't much choice, so he did as he was told, moving slowly and praying the gun wouldn't accidentally discharge.

"Take the car," he stammered, his voice trembling as he fumbled with the seatbelt. "Just take it, but please—leave my son and me alone."

The man, however, didn't seem to have much patience. He grabbed Sandy and yanked him violently, trying to haul him out of the seat. With the seatbelt still in place, it was a futile effort—but the assailant had come prepared. Suddenly, a knife gleamed in his hand.

"No!" Sandy cried, instinctively raising his hands to fend off the attack.

But the man wasn't aiming for his throat. Instead, he slashed the seatbelt with a quick, practiced motion, freeing Sandy from his restraints. Before he could react, the man dragged him out of the car and shoved him toward a van that had pulled up alongside his vehicle.

He was thrown into the van, landing hard on his side. The door slammed shut behind him with a metallic thud.

As he hit the floor, his hip scraped against something cold and unyielding, while his hand slid across a greasy surface. But these minor injuries were the least of his worries.

"Tommy!" he yelled, his voice cracking with panic. "My son!"

The van lurched forward, throwing him back. His head smacked against another unforgiving surface, leaving him dazed. Despite the congested traffic, the van's driver seemed determined to escape at all costs, jumping the curb or mounting the sidewalk.

Shaking off the dizziness, Sandy managed to get to his knees and stumbled toward the partition separating the cargo bay from the driver's cabin. He pounded on it desperately.

"My son! Where is my son?" he shouted, his voice raw with desperation.

But of course there was no response from the thugs in front.

* * *

LORI HARRISON HURRIED to answer the door. The moment she saw the uniformed police officer on her doorstep, she immediately felt a little better.

"Oh, this is just terrible!" she exclaimed as she let the nice man in. "Who would do such a thing?"

"Crooks, ma'am," said the officer as he stepped into Lori's living room. Since she'd never married, it was just her and Melo and Cakes, her beloved Chihuahuas, sharing the house.

"Melo and Cakes are very well-behaved," she assured the officer as she scooped the two tiny doggies into her arms and set them both down in their favorite spot by the window, where they had a perfect view of the street and all its passersby.

The officer glanced around at her antique furniture with an appreciative eye. "Nice place you've got here, ma'am," he said.

"Oh, just call me Lori," she replied. "Unless you're not allowed to? Being a police officer and all?" Even though her brother-in-law was a retired police commissioner and her nephew a serving chief inspector, she was often unsure of the proper etiquette when dealing with the girls and boys in blue. Her nephew was a detective, so he didn't really stand on ceremony. Once, she'd asked her grandniece, who was also a cop, whether they were allowed to accept a drink while on duty. Poppy had laughed and said she had no idea. Lori figured the stuff about not drinking on duty that you saw on TV was probably nonsense.

"Can I offer you something?" she asked, even though she was eager to get down to business.

"No, I'm fine," said the officer, waving a hand.

"So, what's going on?" she asked, gesturing for the officer to take a seat at her dining table. He sat down, placing his cap carefully on the tablecloth. "You told me over the phone there's still a way to retrieve my money?"

"Absolutely," said the officer. "We got there just in time. Now, all we need to do is log into your account to make sure no funny business is taking place. To do that, I'll need your bank card, Ms. Harrison."

She reached for her wallet, which she'd placed on the table in preparation for this visit. Fishing her card out, she handed it over to the officer. "Here you go."

He took it gratefully. "And your PIN code?"

"It's my birthday," she admitted, a little sheepishly. She'd always read that you should make your PIN code as difficult as possible to guess. "Oh-four-five-one."

The officer typed the PIN code into his phone and nodded approvingly at how cooperative she was in providing the information needed to stop the crooks from stealing her money. Probably not everyone was as helpful and prepared as she was.

"So, can you check now?" she asked. "Is everything still there?"

"Let's do that right now," said the officer, pulling a laptop from his bag. It didn't take him long to log into her bank account—certainly much faster than it would take her. But then she didn't use online banking, so she had no idea how it worked, exactly. He certainly made it look easy. He showed her both her checking and savings accounts, and she was immensely relieved to see that all her money was still there—not a single euro missing.

"Oh, thank God," she said, clutching her chest. "What a relief! I really thought they'd taken everything!"

"Looks like we got there just in time," said the officer, fixing her with a stern expression. "Next time someone calls you pretending to be from your bank, hang up straight away, ma'am."

"Oh, I know," she said. "But he sounded so convincing! He said the same thing you just told me—that someone was trying to access my money and I needed to work with him to stop it."

"That's how these people operate," the officer explained. "They scare you into a panic, and then you're like putty in their hands."

"Good thing I don't do my banking online," said Lori. "I told him that, but he wouldn't believe me—at least, not at first. That should have set off all my alarm bells. I mean, if he really worked for my bank, he would've known I don't do online banking. He should've seen it in his system."

"That's probably what saved you," said the officer kindly.

"Oh, I know. Which is why I was so surprised when you called and told me the bank had informed the police that they'd noticed suspicious activity on my account."

"Well, like I always say, better safe than sorry," said the officer as he closed his laptop and stood up.

"I never thought it would happen to me," she admitted with a touch of frustration. "But I guess nobody's immune to these scams."

"The most important thing is that your bank caught on just before these crooks managed to transfer your money," the officer reassured her.

"So, what happens now?" she asked, rising to her feet as well.

"Now, we'll file a report," said the officer. "And, of course, we'll keep you informed every step of the way."

"Will you tell the bank about what happened?"

"Of course. They're the ones who contacted us."

"Thank you so much, officer," she said warmly. "You're very kind."

He grinned, and she noticed a gold tooth near the back of his mouth—a rarity these days, especially for someone as young as he was. "Just doing my job, ma'am."

After she had seen him out, Lori remembered the question she'd meant to ask: Should she have her bank card blocked now? Deciding she could just as easily check with her bank, she picked up her phone and made the call. The line connected to the nice girl who usually sat at the counter when Lori visited. Suzy—that was her name, if she remembered correctly.

"Oh, hi. It's Suzy, right?" she said. "It's Lori Harrison. I just wanted to ask if I need to have my bank card blocked? I mean, this is the first time something like this has happened to me, and I'm not sure what the correct procedure is."

"Correct procedure for what, Ms. Harrison?" Suzy asked, her tone polite but puzzled.

"Well, after you nearly have your money stolen by those nasty crooks, of course." But then Lori realized Suzy might not have been informed about her situation. "You see, I got a phone call from someone claiming to work for my bank. They said there was something strange going on with my bank account and asked if I could log into my banking app to check. Only, I don't use internet banking, so I couldn't log into anything."

"Oh, but Ms. Harrison, you should never do that," Suzy said, suddenly sounding alarmed. "We never call customers and ask them to log into their banking app."

"I know, but this person sounded so professional, so

convincing. It was only when that nice police officer called me right after, saying you'd reported suspicious activity with my account, that I started to worry. And then, when he asked if he could stop by—"

"Ms. Harrison," Suzy interrupted, her tone urgent, "let me check your account real quick, all right?"

"Oh, but you don't have to," Lori said. "The police officer already did that when he was here just now."

For a moment, Suzy was silent. Then she asked, her voice sharp with concern, "Ms. Harrison, did this police officer ask for your PIN code?"

"Well, of course. He needed my bank card and my PIN code to check."

"And you gave them to him?"

For the first time since the police officer had left, Lori experienced a creeping sense of anxiety. "Well... yes."

"Oh, Ms. Harrison," Suzy said, her tone heavy with dread. "I think you'd better come by the bank immediately."

"But... that nice police officer said—"

"Get here as quickly as you can," Suzy said, cutting her off. "I'll try to stop any transactions from going through, but as far as I can tell, your accounts are completely empty."

"Completely... empty?" Lori whispered, the words catching in her throat.

"I'm afraid so," Suzy replied.

"But... how?"

"Can you drop by the bank? Please do it now."

"Yes, of course. I'll be there in twenty minutes."

The moment she hung up, she pressed one of the pre-programmed numbers on her phone. Poppy had set them up for her. It simply read 'Holt.'

CHAPTER 2

*I*t had been a while since Holt had visited his Aunt Lori, and though the circumstances that brought him there now weren't exactly pleasant, he still felt a pang of nostalgia as he stepped inside her cozy apartment. As a boy, he'd spent plenty of time there since Lori had been the designated babysitter for all the kids in the big Holt clan. Having never married, she had always been more than happy to help take care of her family's offspring.

But Holt could see that Aunt Lori wasn't in the mood to reminisce—or to hand out the Melo-Cake chocolate delights she'd been famous for back in the day. Instead, he took a seat at the table and listened patiently as she recounted her tale of woe.

"Police officers *never* drop by to ask for your bank card or your PIN code, Aunt Lori," he said gently. "That is not something we do. *Ever.*"

"How was I supposed to know?" she cried, throwing up her hands in despair. "And now Suzy tells me they might not be able to get my money back! It's all gone! Stolen!"

It really wasn't his job to handle these kinds of situations, so he carefully explained that he'd turn the matter over to the local police, who would try to track down the criminals responsible.

"But he was a *police* officer!" she insisted. "If I describe him to you, surely you'll know who he was, right? He was very young and handsome, and he had a gold tooth."

"That man wasn't actually a police officer, Aunt Lori," he said, his tone firm but kind. "He was pretending to be one to gain your trust and trick you into handing over your bank information."

"Oh, my God!" she said, burying her face in her hands. "And here I thought I was being so clever!"

"These people are professional criminals," Holt explained. "They do this for a living, and they use every trick in the book to fool people into doing what they want."

When Aunt Lori had called him earlier, saying that a police officer was trying to steal her money, he'd immediately contacted his former commissioner at the Loveringem precinct. Ezekiel had sighed heavily, explaining that Aunt Lori wasn't the first victim of this gang—they'd already received several reports earlier that morning about similar scams.

"I'm sure the bank will do everything they can to recover your money," Holt said, placing a reassuring hand on her arm. "Do you want me to ask Mom to drop by?"

Aunt Lori shook her head. "It's all right. I just can't believe how stupid I've been. A fake policeman!" She looked up. "Isn't there a law against impersonating a police officer?"

"There is, and I'm sure Commissioner Forrester and his team will catch them soon enough."

"Oh, God," she said. "He'll make fun of me—I just know he will."

"Who will make fun of you?"

"Your dad, of course! He'll bring this story up at every Christmas from now on."

"I'm sure he won't," said Holt. Although he could already imagine his dad's reaction when he heard his sister-in-law had been duped by a fake cop. Aunt Lori was undoubtedly one of the sweetest people alive, but she also had a bit of a reputation for being a meddler and a busybody—and if there was one thing Holt Sr. hated, it was being told what to do.

"Poppy not with you?" Aunt Lori asked as she picked Melo and Cakes up from the floor and placed the little dogs on her lap. "I thought you two were joined at the hip these days."

"She took a day off," Holt replied with a nod. In truth, Poppy had moved out of the house she and her dad shared and was now living with her new boyfriend. Since she liked things just so, she and the boyfriend were probably at IKEA right now, picking out furniture and curtains and whatnot. But there was no need to share all that with his aunt—besides, he didn't think she was fully aware of Poppy's living arrangements.

"I heard you two were sharing a house?" Aunt Lori asked.

Okay, so maybe she was aware. "We were, but she moved out."

"Living with... what's his name again?"

"Bernard," he replied.

"That's right—Bernard Farre. He owns a restaurant, doesn't he?"

Although Holt had vowed never to speak ill of his daughter's choice of boyfriend, he couldn't help but reply with a touch of scorn, "He doesn't own a restaurant. He's a bartender."

Aunt Lori gave him a sharp look. "You're not thrilled

about him, are you, Glen? Oh, don't deny it. Your mom told me all about it—how you don't think he's good enough for Poppy. And you're probably right. But then nobody will ever be good enough for Poppy."

He shrugged, not wanting to have this conversation. "I guess he's all right."

"After the disaster with her last boyfriend, I just hope this one's a better pick. Our Poppy does have terrible taste in men."

Holt bristled a little. "I wouldn't say that."

"I would, and so would you—if you were being honest."

He shrugged and stood up. "Okay, Ezekiel promised to follow up with you personally. He's sending over two of his officers to take your statement."

Aunt Lori's face clouded. "And how do I know these are real police officers and not more cheaters like the last one?"

"Ask them to produce a badge," he suggested.

"Oh, I wouldn't know a real badge from a fake one. So that won't do me much good."

He smiled. "Maybe it would be best if you simply dropped by the precinct. That way, you won't risk being deceived."

"I probably should have thought of that before I gave that crooked cop all my information." She got up as well and patted his arm. "Thanks for everything, Glen. I know you're a busy man, and you didn't have to come out here for something as minor as your aunt being an old fool."

"You're not an old fool, Aunt Lori," he said firmly. "Plenty of people have been swindled by these crooks. It's really hard these days to know what's real and what's fake."

"I guess so," she said as she walked him to the door. "Give Poppy my love. And tell her to drop by with this new boyfriend of hers. I may not know a fake policeman from a real one, but I like to think I still know how to tell a decent man from a bad apple."

He kissed his aunt on the cheek and promised to pass the message on to his daughter. Though, in truth, he doubted Poppy would take her up on the offer. The last thing she wanted was to trot out Bernard and invite Lori's scrutiny on whether he was a good fit.

CHAPTER 3

*P*oppy stared at the wall, trying to imagine what it would look like with a fresh coat of paint. Bernard didn't care what color she chose and had left it all up to her, figuring she had better taste than he did. She wasn't so sure about that. The last place she had lived—the house she and her dad rented in the pleasant town of Loveringem—hadn't needed much in the way of decoration. The house had been brand-new, and the owner, aided by his wife, a professional interior decorator, had done a stellar job of making it perfectly inhabitable.

Bernard's place, on the other hand, definitely needed a pick-me-up. Or a full makeover. Since she didn't have the faintest idea of where to start, she decided to call in the big guns.

She took out her phone and dialed her mother's number. Mom picked up on the first ring, but before Poppy could explain why she was calling, she exclaimed, "It's serendipity! Or synchronicity! Or both!"

"What is?" she asked, wondering what her mom was talking about.

"You calling at the exact moment I was about to call you!"

"Oh, right. Well, do I go first, or do you?"

"Can I go first, sweetheart? I'm afraid if I wait too long, I'll simply burst!"

"Okay, you go first," Poppy said, walking into the living room and glancing out the window. Bernard was still in bed, fast asleep. As a bartender at one of the town's most popular nightclubs, he spent most nights working and most days asleep. She didn't mind. She wasn't exactly a nine-to-five kind of gal herself. "So, what's the big news?"

"I'm pregnant!"

Whatever she had been expecting, it certainly wasn't that. "You're…"

"Pregnant! Oh, honey, isn't it wonderful? Terrence is over the moon, and so am I!"

"But…"

"Okay, let's talk names," her mom said, cutting her off. "I want you to help me come up with the perfect name. And before you ask, yes, I know if it's a boy or a girl. But I want you to guess."

"Um…"

"It's a girl!"

"You're actually…"

"You're getting a baby sister!"

"Wow. I mean, just… wow."

"It's a miracle, honey. I know we never discussed this, and I'm sure Glen didn't talk to you about it either—that man has always been like a clam when it comes to matters of the heart —but your dad and I, we always said we'd try for a third baby, and we were both hoping it would be a girl. But then we had our little difficulties, and so it never happened. And with Terrence, we never even talked about it, you know, with him having his own kids from his marriage to Melissa, and I wasn't expecting it. It just came out of the blue!"

"It comes out of the blue for me, too," she confessed, taking a seat on the windowsill. "Are you sure, Mom? I mean, have you seen a doctor?"

"Of course I have. You don't think I'd trust one of those silly test things, do you?"

"But I thought that you were... I mean, you told me only last month that..."

"I had entered menopause? That's what I figured, but turns out I was pregnant instead! Isn't it a trip?"

"It sure is," she said, already imagining her dad's face when she told him. Or maybe Mom already had. "Does Dad know?"

"Oh, absolutely not! That man is the absolute last person I'm going to tell. You know what his reaction will be, don't you? Scorn! Mountains of vile ridicule and scorn!"

"I'm sure that Dad will be very happy for you and Terrence, Mom."

"And I'm sure that he won't. But then again, your dad never wanted me to have anything nice. Even when we were married, he went out of his way to make life miserable for me."

"I'm sure that's not the case."

"Let's just leave your dad out of this, shall we?" Mom said in that faux chipper tone she always got when discussing her ex-husband. "He's not going to spoil this sacred moment for me. Not this time. So what do you say, honey?"

"About what?"

"A name, of course. For your baby sister!"

"Um... can I think about it?"

"Absolutely! But don't take too long. I need to have the baby shower invitations printed, the website made, and... oh, there's just a ton of things to do!"

"Maybe you should wait to have the invitations printed? I mean, it's early days, isn't it? And at your age—"

"What is that supposed to mean?" Mom demanded, her voice rising about an octave. "I'm only forty-five! I'm in the prime of my life! My best years are still ahead of me!"

"Of course. I just meant that pregnancies get more complicated as you get older."

"I know that," she said snippily. "And I can assure you that Dr. Osgood has everything well in hand. He even told me that he'd never seen a vagina as beautiful as mine."

"That's... disturbing," Poppy said, making a mental note never to pick Dr. Osgood as her OB/GYN.

"I want you to promise me one thing, Poppy."

"What?"

"Don't tell your dad about this, all right? I want him to hear it from me first."

"But I thought you said Dad would be the absolute last person in the world you would tell?"

"And he will be. But I'll have to tell him at some point. You know what that man is like. He has a knack for finding out stuff."

That's probably because he's a detective, Poppy thought. "Better not wait too long, Mom. He has a right to know."

"No, he doesn't. He lost the right to control me the moment he signed the divorce papers."

Poppy could see that, in spite of her mom's protestations that she didn't want to discuss her ex-husband, somehow the conversation always drifted back to him.

"So what did you want to talk to me about?" Mom asked.

"Oh. Well, the thing is, Bernard and I are sprucing up the apartment a little, and you know I have absolutely no talent in that department, Mom, so I was hoping you might be able to give us some advice?"

"Ooh, I'd love nothing more," Mom said, as Poppy had hoped she would. "Are you at the apartment now?"

"Yep, I'm here, and so is Bernard." She didn't mention that

her boyfriend was asleep. For some reason, her parents hadn't quite taken to Bernard yet, with her dad simply staring at her in that disconcerting way he had when she broke the news to him, and Mom not taking too well to the news that her daughter's new boyfriend was a bartender at a nightclub.

"Okay, I'll be there in twenty minutes," said Mom. "And then we can go shopping for curtains together. We'll have so much fun!"

Only Mom could possibly think that shopping for curtains was fun, but Poppy was so grateful for her input that instead she said, "Yep. It'll be a hoot."

"And while we're at it, I want to drop by the store for baby clothes."

"Couldn't you use my old clothes?" asked Poppy.

The tinkling laugh on the other end of the line spoke volumes. Recycling old clothes was not her mother's way. And besides, she probably had thrown them all away years ago.

After she hung up the phone, Bernard came drifting into the room. He was yawning and his hair stood up in weird peaks. "Was that your mom?" he asked.

"Yeah, she's pregnant," she said.

It was a testament to the fact that he had only just woken up that he didn't even react to that piece of monumental news. "Great stuff," he said instead. He slouched into the kitchen. "Is there any coffee left?"

"Just pop a capsule into the coffee maker," she said. Like her boyfriend, she was a big coffee drinker and could go through a liter a day if she didn't pace herself. In that sense, they were fully compatible. "Mom is coming over," she announced.

In the process of selecting a coffee capsule, he froze and slowly turned to her, gulping. "Your mom is coming over?"

"We're going shopping," she said as blithely as she could. "For curtains."

"Oh, great," he said. "I don't have to come, right?"

"No, you don't have to come," she assured him. He looked so relieved that it was almost comical. The lack of affection between her parents and Bernard clearly wasn't a one-way street. He didn't much care for them either. Then again, after the way they had stared at him when she had first introduced him to them, that wasn't hard to understand. Dad had been the worst, putting on his best cop face when she had brought Bernard home one night and told her dad he was her new boyfriend. On the verge of giving him a first-degree interrogation, she actually had to stop him in his tracks and remind him that they weren't at the precinct and that Bernard wasn't a suspect in some heinous crime.

Afterward, Bernard and her dad had sat on the couch together while Poppy messed around in the kitchen, trying to whip up something edible. Her idea had been to allow the two some bonding time, but that hadn't happened. Instead, Dad had started firing off questions at Bernard, and the poor boy had clammed up. So much for male bonding.

At her mom's place, they hadn't fared much better, with Terrence looking at Bernard like something the cat had regurgitated on the floor, and Mom reacting exactly like her usual self when Bernard's profession had been mentioned.

"A bartender!" she had exclaimed, as if it was the worst job in the world, up there with drug dealer and hitman.

The worst moment had come when Terrence had taken her aside and suggested he run a background check on Bernard. Unfortunately, the latter had been within earshot and had blanched when he realized he was about to be run through the police database like a common criminal.

Suffice it to say, they hadn't repeated the experience.

Bernard sipped from his cup of coffee and glanced

around the room. "Maybe we should clean up a little?" he suggested. "Before your mom gets here and throws a hissy fit?"

He was barefoot and dressed in his boxer shorts and Dimitri Vegas & Like Mike T-shirt, looking so cute that Poppy could have gobbled him up. Even though they had only been together a couple of weeks, she was still as much in love as the first time they'd met, at the same club where he worked. She'd been out with a couple of friends after a reunion party at her old school, and even though he'd behaved like an absolute gentleman throughout the evening, it hadn't escaped her attention—or that of her friends—that he had taken an instant liking to her. Maybe the little notes he added to the drinks she ordered gave it away. He had added things like 'To the cutest girl in the house' or 'To the sexiest redhead alive.'

He wasn't exactly subtle. But it didn't matter. It had done the trick, for when the evening wound down, and he informed her that his shift ended at four, they walked home together—to his apartment—and she ended up staying the night.

She probably should have told her dad, though, because when she woke up in the morning and checked her phone, she had about a thousand messages from him, demanding to know where she was. He had been on the verge of sending out a search team when she called and told him she was fine.

The doorbell rang, and she glanced out of the window to see her mom down below on the sidewalk, waving at her. She was dressed in an actual pink fur coat, with her fancy Jaguar parked haphazardly across the curb, blocking foot traffic.

Bernard, who had joined her, stood there with his mouth open. "Is that... a mink coat? Isn't that, like, illegal or something?"

"Not to Mom, it isn't," she said. She gave her boyfriend a quick kiss on the lips, which then turned into something a lot less quick and lingering, and finally managed to extricate herself and tell him that she'd be back soon—loaded with curtains.

"Can't wait," he said with a grin.

CHAPTER 4

*H*olt was on his way home when a call came in. He checked his phone and saw that his daughter was trying to reach him. He clicked a button on the steering wheel, and Poppy's voice echoed through the car. "Hey, Dad. What's all this about Aunt Lori being robbed?"

"Yeah, she was scammed. A guy impersonating a police officer convinced her she needed to hand over her bank card and PIN code."

"And she did?" Poppy sounded incredulous.

"She did, yeah."

"Oh, God. I must have told her a million times never to give any of her personal information to anyone."

"And still she did." He entered the street where he and Poppy used to live. "I've handed it to the local plods. They should be able to get a bead on these people. Apparently, they've been pretty busy scamming elderly folks in Aunt Lori's neighborhood."

He grabbed his phone from the holder and got out of the car. Walking up to the house, he suddenly remembered he should have picked up Harley from his parents. He leaned against the car. "So how is the redecorating going? Have you guys picked the wallpaper yet?"

"I told you this, Dad. We're not going to wallpaper. We'll stick with painting."

He smiled a wry sort of smile. He probably should be more involved in his daughter's redecoration project, but since he couldn't hide the fact that he wasn't fully on board with her choice of a new boyfriend, he had a hard time showing any excitement for the big move. And also, even though he'd never admit it to anyone, least of all Poppy herself, he missed having her around at home. Now they only saw each other at work, like regular colleagues. It had been great to cook for her and to talk shop at the dinner table. Oh, well.

"There's one other thing I needed to talk to you about, Dad," she said.

Uh-oh. "What's that?" She was quiet for a moment, and he frowned. "Sounds like it's pretty important?" Surely she wasn't getting married to this fool? Or having his baby? The thought of welcoming Bernard into the family as his son-in-law wasn't the greatest of prospects. If possible, he liked the guy even less than Rupert, Poppy's last boyfriend.

But as he mentally braced himself for the shock announcement, instead, she said, "It's Mom."

"Your mom? What's wrong with her?"

She sighed. "Look, she probably won't like me telling you this, but I get the feeling she'll never get around to it, so I figure you might as well hear it from me instead."

"Hear what?" A million scenarios ran through his mind, from the worst to the horrendous. But then something occurred to him. "Are she and Terrence getting a divorce?"

"No, Dad. They're going to be parents."

What she said didn't quite compute. "I don't understand," he confessed.

"Mom is pregnant."

It was a good thing that he was leaning against the hood of the car, or he might have fallen over. "Pregnant? But how?"

Poppy laughed. "Dad, you're a little old for the birds and bees story. How do you think it happened?"

"But... your mom is..." He had to be careful what he said here. "Not young."

"She's forty-five. And according to her gynecologist, everything is fine and she'll be able to carry the baby to term."

Now that was the kind of news that got you reeling. "I didn't even know they were trying for a baby."

"They weren't. It took them as much by surprise as it does you—or me. But it's happening."

"A baby," he said. "Well, how about that?"

"Okay, I've gotta go. Mom is trying on maternity dresses, and she just walked out of the fitting room." She promptly hung up, and for a moment Holt just stood there. Faint recollections of Leah breaking the news to him that she was pregnant with Poppy flitted through his mind, and a sort of sad feeling assaulted him. Something about opportunities squandered and all of that. He quickly stomped down on them. He'd never been a sentimental man, and he wasn't going to let this news affect him too much. Instead, he got back into his car and drove over to his parents' place to pick up his dog.

Harley greeted him with an adorable peeping sound and his tail wagging excitedly, as he always did when Holt showed up.

He bent down and accepted a couple of licks across the face. "Good boy," he said affectionately. "Did you miss me? Huh? I sure missed you, Harley."

"He always misses you," said Holt's mom as she wiped her

hands on her apron. "Wanna stay for dinner? We haven't eaten yet."

"Sure," he said. Now that Poppy had left, dinnertime wasn't as much fun as it used to be, and so he often had dinner at his parents' place instead. He followed his mom into the kitchen, Harley jumping up against his leg all the while. "Maybe I better take him for a walk first."

"He's been waiting for you. Sitting in the window for the past hour and not moving an inch."

Dad was seated at the kitchen table reading a magazine and looked up when his son entered the room. "Hey, Dad," he said and clapped the old man affectionately on the back. "Did you hear about Aunt Lori?"

"Heard all about it," said his dad, who was a retired police commissioner and had once upon a time headed up the local police department. "Ezekiel called me personally and promised to keep me in the loop as they try to track down these hoodlums." He shook his head. "If I've told that woman once never to give her PIN code to a stranger, I've told her a million times."

"Lori is too trusting," said Mom as she checked something in the oven that smelled pretty darn delicious. "Is it true that the thief was dressed as a police officer?"

"Yeah, he was," said Holt. He wondered if he should tell his folks about Leah being pregnant, but decided that maybe he should hold off on that for now. Maybe over dinner.

"What a rotten thing to do," said Mom, "to pretend to be a cop, the one person people are supposed to trust more than anyone in the world. No wonder Lori was fooled."

"She shouldn't have been," Dad said. "No police officer will ever ask you for your PIN code. Why would they? What could they possibly need your PIN code for?"

"I'm sure that Ezekiel will catch these people soon

enough," said Mom. She directed a keen look at her son. "How is Poppy settling in?"

"Oh, fine," said Holt in the sort of breezy tone that didn't quite become him. "Yeah, she's busy redecorating, you know."

"Have you met this young man of hers?" asked Dad.

"Um, yeah," he admitted. "Yeah, she introduced us."

"And?" asked Mom eagerly. "What is he like?"

"Um..." He glanced down at Harley, who was eyeing him affectionately and with an eagerness that was endearing to see. He patted the French bulldog on the head. "Why don't I take Harley for that walk now, and then I'll tell you all about it over dinner."

Mom's face clouded. "That bad, huh?"

"Oh, no," he assured her. "I'm sure he's a fine young man."

Mom shook her head. "One thing I've always admired about you, Glen, is that you're such a great judge of character. And if you don't think this young man is good enough for our Poppy, then he's not good enough for her." She sank down on a chair. "She's going to get her heart broken all over again, isn't she?"

"But I never said..."

"And one other thing I know about you, Glen Holt," said Mom, wagging a finger in his face, "is that you would have made a lousy poker player. I can see it on your face that you hate this new boyfriend of Poppy's. Don't you dare deny it!"

He raised his shoulders. "I only met the guy once!"

"Once is enough," said Mom determinedly. She actually gave her son an accusing look now. "Why did you allow this, Glen? Why didn't you protect your daughter from this boy?"

"I'm sure that it's not like that, Bettina," Dad said. "Poppy is a big girl, and she knows better than to get involved with just anyone. Isn't that right, son?"

"Absolutely," said Holt. "If Poppy thinks this guy is the one—"

"The one!" Mom cried as she raised her hands in despair. "Did she actually call him that? This is worse than I thought!"

"Okay, I'm going to walk the dog now," said Holt.

"You do that," said Dad. The old man actually had a twinkle in his eyes as he gave him a wink. "And your mom and I will think of a way to save Poppy from disaster."

"You always make fun of me," Mom complained. "But if Poppy's heart gets broken again, it's your fault," she said, pointing a finger in Holt's direction. "And also yours!"

"How is Poppy's love life suddenly my responsibility?" asked Dad.

Holt decided to leave his parents to discuss the ins and outs of their granddaughter's love life while he took Harley for his walk. He figured he'd probably keep that other little nugget about Leah being pregnant to himself for now. No need to upset his mom even more than she already was.

As he and his trusty canine walked the block, he found his mind turning back to the events of the past couple of months. After the success he'd had bringing to justice the murderer of Mayor Jan Birt, the powers that be had determined that maybe Holt's abilities were being wasted in Loveringem, and they had offered him a promotion that would propel him back to where the action was: Ghent. This time he wouldn't be working for his old boss Terrence Bayton, coincidentally also Leah's new husband, but for the Federal Police. And since he was extremely proud of his team, he'd suggested that they be promoted along with him— if they were up for it. Poppy jumped at the chance, and much to his surprise, so did the rest of the team: Georgina, Leland, and Rasheed had all joined him at the Groendreef, located in the north of Ghent and conveniently far away from his old precinct at Ekkergem.

The only inconvenience was that he had to drive into

Ghent every day from Loveringem, but he was already looking for new lodgings closer to police headquarters.

Harley was sniffing here and there and doing his business wherever he saw fit when all of a sudden Holt saw a guy get out of a car ahead of him, dressed in a police uniform. He frowned, for he knew all the local cops, and he had never seen this guy before. And then it hit him: the guy perfectly matched the description that Aunt Lori had given him.

This was the guy—the thief!

As Holt was nearing, the guy happened to look behind him. For a moment, his eyes locked with Holt's, and what he must have seen there must have scared the living daylights out of him, for he suddenly broke into a run. Holt growled, "Get him, Harley. Get that guy!" and set off after the guy himself.

Harley might not be a police dog and was probably too small to harbor any ambitions of ever becoming one, but what he did have was the bulldog's instinct for catching his man.

The dog didn't need to be told twice and had shot away from Holt like a bullet from a gun, chasing after the crook at full blast. Moments later, he was propelling himself through the air and expertly attached himself to the man's behind, clinging there as if he'd never done anything else his entire life.

"Eek!" the crook yelped as the mighty jaws of the bulldog closed on his tushy.

The intervention broke the man's stride, and already Holt was upon him, dragging him down and sitting across his back so he didn't get any funny ideas. "You can let go now, Harley," he said. And when the dog didn't obey, he added, "Let go!"

This time Harley did let go, but not before ripping a piece of fabric from the man's standard-issue police pants and settling down with the swath of dark blue fabric between his teeth. He had a look of intense satisfaction on his face.

"That dog is a menace!" said the crook. "It should be put down!"

"You're under arrest, son," said Holt as he produced his police badge.

The guy checked the badge. "Is that for real?"

Holt could see how he would think that, being a fake police officer himself, he was being arrested by a fake police officer. "Yeah, it's for real. Now let's get you booked in, buddy."

"I wanna press charges," said the guy, who was very young, Holt thought. Early twenties at the most. "Police violence."

"Yeah, yeah," said Holt. "Save it for the judge."

CHAPTER 5

*R*asheed frowned at his screen. He had just managed to lose two games in a row against his opponent, MikeJam89.

"Dammit," he muttered as he lowered his controller. Normally, he was so good at this, but for some reason, this MikeJam89 kept kicking his ass.

A tap on his shoulder lifted him from his reverie. It was Georgina, one of his housemates. He lifted his headphones away from his ear.

"We're leaving," she said. "Last chance to change your mind."

"Nah, I'm good," he said.

Behind Georgina, Leland made a face.

"Are you sure?" he asked. "It's gonna be epic, bro. We're hitting the Marquee tonight."

"Nah, you go and have fun," he said. Even though he hated to explain why, he had never enjoyed the particular ambiance you find in a nightclub. The loud music, the stench, the crowd. Not to mention the exorbitant prices of the drinks. Rasheed didn't drink, and to pay five bucks for a Pepsi he could enjoy at home for a fraction of the cost was simply ludicrous. His beleaguered bank account would bitch and moan if he joined his colleagues at the club.

"Oh, you can bet we'll have fun!" said Leland as he comically wiggled his eyebrows.

"Okay, behave, all right?" said Georgina as she placed a hand on his shoulder. She gave him a worried look, the way she always did when he preferred to stay home and play video games rather than go out with them.

The moment the door was closed, he picked up his game controller again, but just at that moment, his phone chimed, and he picked it up from the desk. When he saw that it was his mom, his heart sank. But since he couldn't not pick up, he thumbed the green button.

"Mom, what's up?" he said.

"What's up?" Mom said. "Is that a way to greet your mother?"

"I'm sorry, Mom," he said, not wanting to get into an argument with his mom. He needed to get back to the game and make sure he didn't get his ass kicked by MikeJam89 again. Even if he had to play all night, he was going to get his revenge!

"When are you going to move out of there?" Mom demanded.

He rolled his eyes. God, not this nonsense again. "I'm not moving out, Mom. I only just moved in, so that would be silly."

"You are living in sin, Rasheed!" she cried.

"I'm not living in sin," he said. "All I'm doing is sharing a house with a couple of my colleagues, that's all."

"And one of them just so happens to be an unmarried woman! You are living under the same roof as an unmarried woman! To my mind, that's living in sin."

"Mom…"

"I want you to move out of there."

"I told you. I can't afford to rent a place of my own right now. Ghent is expensive."

"Then you move away from Ghent."

"Then I'd need to commute every day, which is a real drag."

He'd considered commuting and staying at the apartment he had rented before, near Loveringem. But spending over an hour in traffic every day was bullshit, and so when Georgina and Leland, who were struggling with the same issue, had suggested the three of them rent a place together for the time being, he'd jumped at the chance. As luck would have it, a close friend of Georgina's grandparents had recently passed away and had decided to leave the house that they'd lived in all their lives to their granddaughter. And since she already owned a place of her own, she had decided to rent it out—preferably to someone she knew and trusted. Like Georgina.

It had been perfect. Exactly what they wanted. And so they had all moved in over a single weekend, with each one occupying a room on a different floor, while they shared the bathroom and the kitchen. They'd drawn up a schedule for the cleaning, and so far so good. They even had a common space where they could watch television, though to be honest, Rasheed spent most of his time in his room playing video games. They did eat dinner together, even though the cooking situation was in something of a flux right now. None of them were exactly proficient at cooking, so for now, they mostly bought ready-made meals they only had to shove into the microwave. Leland was going to take cooking lessons, though, so things were looking up. Or not, depending on how talented Leland proved to be.

"Look, I can't afford a place of my own right now," said

Rasheed, who was getting sick and tired of this constant nagging from his mom. "And I don't want to move back in with you guys either," he quickly added before his mom could make the suggestion again. He was too old to live with his parents. Imagine the grief they'd give him over his video games. Or his job. They'd probably want him to quit the force as well, as they'd never been fully on board with his choice of career.

"All I'm saying is that you can't live under the same roof as that girl," said Mom, trying to sound reasonable but coming off like a lunatic. "She's a Jezebel, and she's tainting you with her... Jezebelness."

He laughed. "You just made that up."

"Okay, so maybe I made it up," she admitted. "But she's still a Jezebel, and you shouldn't allow her to try and seduce you."

"She's not trying to seduce me, Mom. And besides, Georgina is not my type. Like, at all."

The only male under this roof that Georgina should be wary of was Leland, but then he wasn't Georgina's type, so that was only ever going to happen in Leland's dreams.

"Okay, but at least you have to promise me that you will lock your room at night. So she can't sneak into your bed."

"Georgina isn't the sneaking-into-bed type of person, Mom," he said.

"Are you still using the same bathroom?"

"Yes, Mom. There's only the one bathroom, so we have to share that."

"Before you take a shower, make sure you clean it well. Use plenty of disinfectant. You never know where this girl has been."

The conversation went on like that for a while, but in the end, Mom gave up, and he could finally get back to his game.

And so he cracked his knuckles and picked up the controller. "Expect to get your ass kicked, MikeJam89," he growled. Before long, he was back in business.

CHAPTER 6

*L*eland loved this new setup. Not only did he get to live in close proximity to the object of his affections, but he also got to spend his nights clubbing with her. In other words: a dream come true. Even though he had managed to keep his affection for his colleague hidden from everyone, he still figured he'd have more of a chance now that they shared a house. After all, even though they weren't a couple, they actually lived together. Which was just so cool! Everything he had always hoped for had been dropped into his lap.

And all because he and the rest of the team had caught Jan Birt's killer when no one believed they could do it. Even Holt's old chief had figured he had Birt's killer nabbed when he hadn't. A fine revenge for Holt against his old nemesis.

He watched as Georgina sashayed back to the table, holding the drinks they had ordered. She had spent far too long chatting up the bartender to his liking, but then he had to admit that the guy was pretty hot—if you were into the whole dark and mysterious stranger thing. He had plenty of piercings and tattoos all over the parts of his body that were on display. Did Georgina like that kind of thing? If so, maybe he should get some tats. Piercings were a different matter. He couldn't very well go around with nose studs and stuff. Even though Holt probably wouldn't mind, the top brass would.

The night was young, and the place wasn't exactly rocking yet, but it wouldn't be long before it was. The Marquee was the hottest club in town, located in the Overpoort neighborhood, and got plenty of buzz.

He accepted his drink from Georgina and gave her a grateful smile. "What did he have to say?" he asked, raising his voice over the noise of the music. It was some kind of techno beat. Not exactly his favorite, but then that couldn't be helped. It was Georgina's favorite, so a small sacrifice for him to make.

"Oh, nothing special," said Georgina as she took a sip from her drink. "There's this great DJ coming in a little later. DJ Smurf. Supposed to be one of the best at the moment."

Leland grimaced. "What genre?"

"Mh? Oh, techno. What else?"

He should have known. He was going to have to listen to this crap all night, wasn't he?

She must have seen the look on his face, for she asked, "Why? You don't like it?"

"Oh, I love it!" he said, trying to project the requisite level of excitement. "So groovy!"

She laughed. "Groovy! Who went and transported you back to the sixties, bud?" She nudged his shoulder. "Look, I know you prefer heavy metal, so why don't we check out some heavy metal joint later on?" His face must have revealed his true convictions, for she laughed again. "I knew you hated techno."

"I don't hate it," he said. "I just... well, it's always the same, isn't it? Dunka dunka dunka. On and on."

"Of course it is," she said with a grin. She studied him for a moment. "You know, you don't look like a metalhead. I mean, where are the tats, the metal, the funky outfits, huh?"

He shrugged. "When you're a cop, you can't exactly express yourself the way you would like." Though the truth was that he might be a metalhead, he'd never been a big fan of the lifestyle. For him, it was all about the music, not the looks.

And he was just going to suggest they don't stick around for this cool DJ when Georgina took her phone out of her pocket. The way she was frowning at the device told him that something was up. "What's wrong?" he asked.

"Remember Jeanine?" she asked.

"Sure." Jeanine was their landlord, so to speak—the friend who was renting out her grandparents' house.

"She's been spiked," said Georgina, sliding down from her stool. "Let's go."

"Where is she?" he asked.

"Right outside," she said.

"When did this happen?"

"Just now."

Georgina led the way to the back of the club, and as she shoved open the emergency exit, she almost hit a bouncer in the back of the head. He looked up, annoyed by her sudden emergence on the scene. But when he saw it was her, he quickly simmered down. Everyone knew Georgina, who'd been a big fan of clubbing ever since she was old enough to go out.

They found Jeanine sitting on the sidewalk, her head in her hands. She'd obviously been crying. She looked up when Georgina and Leland approached and held out her arms.

Georgina gave the stricken girl a hug. She was dressed the same way Georgina was: in her best clubbing attire, though her makeup was streaked, and she looked terrible.

"What do you remember?" asked Georgina.

"Not much," said the young woman. "I was in there, waiting for you guys to show up, when I had to go to the bathroom. Then, when I was in there, I suddenly felt woozy and weird, and the next thing I remember, I passed out."

"Spiked," Georgina confirmed. "Were you interfered with, you think?"

"I'm not sure," said the woman as she wiped her nose with her sleeve. "Like I said, I don't remember much."

"Did someone offer you a drink?" asked Leland.

The girl shook her head. "I don't think so. Like I said, I was waiting for you guys to show up. I only did have the one drink—at least I think I did." She frowned and screwed her eyes closed. "It's just one big blur, you know."

"We'd better get you to a hospital," said Georgina. "And have you checked out. Is that all right with you, Jeanine?"

The girl nodded. "Yeah, I think that's probably for the best."

There had been a spate of spiking in the area lately, and this seemed to be just the latest one. Pity it wasn't on the Federal Police's radar, so they wouldn't be able to pursue the case even if they wanted to. But what they could do was make sure that Jeanine was taken care of and had all the support she needed. Leland really liked the girl, and not just because she was one of Georgina's friends and had given them a roof over their heads. She was genuinely good people and didn't deserve this nonsense.

As Georgina called in the incident, Leland sat with Jeanine. "Did you leave your drink unattended?" he asked.

She shook her head. "You know, I've told friends to watch out for this shit so many times. And then it happens to me." She thunked her head with her fist. "Stupid. So stupid."

"Hey, don't say that. You're not the one responsible for this. The person who spiked your drink is. This wasn't your fault."

"Yeah, I guess." She frowned. "I don't think he did anything to me, though. I mean, I was in the toilet when I passed out. It was only the banging on the door that woke me up, and the stall door was still closed. It's just that I was still feeling out of it when I stumbled out here. But if he had done something to me, I would have noticed, don't you think?"

"Best to have you checked out anyway," he advised.

He saw that Georgina was talking to the bouncer, probably asking him if he saw something. When she returned, she was smiling. "Mike says that from the moment you walked out, he had his eye on you, and nothing happened. He also says you were in the bathroom an awfully long time, so they got worried and banged on the door and that's when you came out. So looks like you're safe, babe."

"Oh, thank God," said Jeanine. She shivered. "It's so scary, you know. To lose all control like that? Just the absolute worst feeling in the world."

"I know," said Georgina as she took a seat next to her friend and placed an arm around her shoulder to pull her close. As Leland watched the two women he probably liked the most in the world, a sudden sensation of helplessness assaulted him, followed by a flare-up of unadulterated anger at the person who would spike a girl's drink hoping to get into her panties. What kind of monster did such a thing?

CHAPTER 7

*C*ommissioner Garrett Simpson sat with his eyes closed, his brow furrowed like a corrugated roof. Finally, he opened his eyes again and fixed them on his audience, which consisted of Holt and his team, present and accounted for in the commissioner's office.

"Right," said the commissioner. He blinked a few times, as if trying to remember what he'd been in the process of saying.

"The kidnapping, sir?" Holt suggested.

"Right, right. The kidnapping indeed. So the case has been dropped in our laps, as local police seem to feel there might be more to this than meets the eye."

"What does that mean, sir?" asked Poppy. Holt noticed that she was sitting, eager as always, her pen poised over her notebook.

"Well, as you know, when Doctor McMinn was taken, he wasn't alone in the car. His five-year-old son Tommy was strapped in his safety seat in the back. So local plod figured they'd return the child to his mother for the time being. Only they discovered that the mother is in a mental hospital. She's been committed."

"Committed?" asked Holt.

"By her own husband, apparently. For some reason, the good doctor felt the need to have his wife admitted to the loonie bin. And that's not all. According to witnesses, the kidnapping was executed to perfection. Looked like a professional hit. And that's why the powers that be decided to transfer Sandy McMinn's abduction to us. They figure there might be a connection to organized crime."

"Okay, we'll get on it, sir," said Holt, getting up.

"Oh, and Holt?" said the commissioner, holding up his hand. "Please be tactful. Try not to act like a bull in a china shop."

"Understood, sir," said Holt. He'd heard this speech so many times it was practically a given that he'd be reminded of it at the start of every single one of his investigations.

* * *

POPPY WONDERED how much they'd learn from this visit. As far as she could tell, patients at these mental institutions were often kept under sedation. If that was true about Clarissa McMinn, the interview would be a very short one. Then again, if they didn't try, they wouldn't know.

"Have you ever been here, Dad?" she asked as she tried to keep up with her father.

"Once," he admitted. "Aunt Gardenia, when Uncle Luther died, went through a difficult time, and so it was decided to have her admitted for her own protection. She wasn't here long, though. Just a couple of weeks, if I remember correctly."

"I didn't know that," Poppy admitted. But then there were

probably a lot of things about her own family that she wasn't aware of. These types of things were mostly not talked about in front of the kids. And as she had only been a young girl when her dad's uncle died, they wouldn't have mentioned it to her. She wouldn't have understood the significance anyway. "By the way, how is Aunt Lori? Did she get her money back?"

"Not yet," said her dad. "Though they did manage to catch the entire gang, apparently."

"Harley did good," she said. And when he gave her a look, she quickly added, "And so did you, Dad. You caught the guy."

"Well, to be honest, it's true that Harley did most of the work. When that guy met the business end of Harley's teeth, he had already lost."

Poppy laughed. "I would have loved to have seen that. Harley in action. That must have been quite the sight."

"Oh, it was," said her dad with a grin.

They had reached the main vestibule of the psychiatric hospital and announced their presence. The receptionist told them to take a seat in the waiting area, and so they did.

"It certainly doesn't look like a mental hospital," said Poppy. It was a very airy and bright vestibule, with plenty of glass and lots of greenery. "More like a luxury hotel."

"Wait till you see the rooms," said Holt. "They're very nice. Like you said, more like a luxury hotel than a clinic. But then this place is probably the most expensive one in town."

"How come the family could afford to send Aunt Gardenia here?"

"Uncle Luther had been pretty well off. He owned a candy factory that was very successful—and still is. These days it's run by cousin Francis and his wife."

A man with an impressive white beard approached the reception desk, and as the receptionist pointed in the direction where Holt and Poppy were waiting, he turned and smiled, then came walking over. "Chief Inspector Holt?" he asked as he shook Holt's hand.

"And this is Inspector Holt," said Holt. "She's my daughter," he added in answer to the unspoken question.

"Father and daughter, fighting crime together," said the doctor, looking amused. "That's so wonderful. My name is Shawn Luukkonen, by the way. I run this facility. I understand you would like to talk to one of my patients?"

"Yes. Clarissa McMinn's husband has been abducted. And we're talking to everyone in Doctor McMinn's life."

"Yes, I heard about that," said the doctor, a frown of concern marring his smooth features. He had a long square beard that reminded Poppy of the late King Leopold II. "Terrible business. Absolutely terrible. But I'm afraid I can't allow you to talk to Mrs. McMinn. She's still in a bad way and can't be subjected to any kind of interrogation."

"It's just an interview," Holt corrected the medical man.

"I'm afraid I can't give you permission to talk to my patient," said the doctor, more adamant this time. His beard waggled energetically. "She's not in the frame of mind to talk to anyone—least of all a pair of police detectives."

"Why was she admitted?" asked Holt.

"I'm afraid I can't divulge a patient's medical history. Let's just say her husband was concerned that she might pose a risk both to herself and her young son. Her primary care physician agreed and so he got the ball rolling on having her committed to this facility."

"She was a danger to her son?" asked Poppy, aghast.

The doctor nodded mournfully. "She was."

"So she didn't admit herself?" asked Holt.

"No, she did not. She was committed."

"By her primary care practitioner?"

"I can give you his name if you like. Though I don't see

the relevance to your investigation into her husband's kidnapping."

Under normal circumstances, Holt would have said it was his business to decide if something was relevant to his investigation or not, but possibly remembering the words of the commissioner, he simply said, "We believe there's a chance it might be."

"Very well," said the doctor, though he didn't look convinced. "That would be Doctor Singh. Judson Singh."

"Perfect," Holt assured the man, whose smile had returned.

Once they were outside, Poppy turned to her dad. "Does this smell fishy to you, too?"

"It does," he confirmed. "He was suspiciously reticent, our Doctor Luukkonen."

CHAPTER 8

*W*anda Gaughan welcomed them into her home with a warmth they usually weren't awarded by the people they paid a visit. But then, when they were settled in her living room and she started talking, Holt understood why.

"He did this," she said viciously.

He quirked an eyebrow. "He being...?"

"Sandy, of course. That no-good scum had her committed so he could take my nephew."

"But... why would he do that?" asked Poppy the obvious question.

"Because she was going to divorce him and take Tommy, of course." She drew a hand across her brow. She looked tired, Holt determined, clearly sick with worry over her sister. "That marriage was doomed from the start. I told Clarissa from the beginning that Sandy was not the right man for her. But of course, she wouldn't listen. She was smitten with the guy, taken in by all of his bullshit. Oh, he's a smooth talker, and charming when he wants to be. But deep down, he's got a heart of stone. All he ever wanted was a maid and a woman who would give him a child, and he got all of that from Clarissa. Until she understood that there was no affection in the marriage. Sandy isn't capable of it. That's the simple truth."

"And so he had her committed to the psychiatric hospital?" asked Poppy.

Wanda nodded. "The director there is a close friend of Sandy's. He's got this funny name, um… Shawn something."

"Shawn Luukkonen?" asked Holt.

"Yeah, something like that. He and Sandy went to medical school together. And also that quack who provided the medical prescription that got my sister committed."

"Doctor Singh."

"They're all in on it together. It's a conspiracy, chief inspector. They all ganged up on my sister when she told Sandy that she wanted a divorce. He must have understood that she was going to get custody of the boy and decided to put a stop to it. Make sure that wasn't happening. And it won't. He'll argue she's in no fit state to get custody."

"But surely he can't get away with this," said Poppy.

"Oh, watch him. That man is as devious as they come."

"Well, he's been abducted," said Holt. "So he won't get away with anything right now." He directed a scrutinizing look at the woman. "Can you tell us where you were yesterday morning, Mrs. Gaughan? Let's say around eight-thirty?"

She gave him a look of astonishment. "You're not seriously accusing me of kidnapping my brother-in-law, are you? I may never have liked the guy, but I'm not in the business of kidnapping people. Even though he hurt my sister."

"Just tell us where you were, please," said Poppy.

"At the daycare," said the woman, her lips forming a straight line. She wasn't as happy with them as she had been before. "I run a daycare in the Rabot neighborhood. Just ask the parents of the kids. They usually start dropping them off at seven, and I was right there."

"Why did your sister decide to divorce her husband?" asked Holt. "Was there a specific reason why now?"

The woman nodded. "He hit her. It had never happened before, mind you. He was always violent, but only verbally. The vile things that slid from that man's serpent tongue... But he was never physically violent. Until he was. And so she knew she had to get away from him. Not just for her sake, but also for Tommy. What if he got violent with him, too? Started smacking him around? She had always said that if he raised a single finger against her, she would leave him, and he knew she was true to her word. He begged her for forgiveness, but she was implacable. We both grew up in a violent home, you see, and she didn't want that for herself or for her son. Nor me, for that matter," she added. "But fortunately, I married a sweet man who would never hurt a soul." As she walked them to the door, she asked, a pleading note in her voice, "Isn't there anything you can do to get my sister out of that place? She doesn't belong there. I know for a fact that whatever they say she's suffering from is a lie. Her place is at home, with her son. Especially now that Sandy has been taken."

"I'll look into it," Holt promised, even though he didn't think there was a lot he could do. Admissions to psychiatric hospitals did sometimes occur with the involvement of the police, but when the reason for the admission was medical, a police report wouldn't do much to convince them otherwise. But that didn't mean he couldn't at least try.

As he settled into the passenger seat and Poppy climbed behind the wheel, he got a call from Aunt Lori. He put the phone on speaker and picked up with a cheerful, "How are you, Aunt Lori?"

47

"Oh, I'm fine," she assured him. "And you know what? I got my money back!"

"You did? That's great."

"Yeah, the bank manager called me personally to give me the news. Said they'd managed to stop the money from leaving my account or something. I don't understand half of it, but the part I do understand is that I've got my money back. Or at least I will when they finally get around to depositing it into my account. I checked at the bank just now, and it's not there yet, even though the manager promised. But the girl at the counter said that sometimes it can take a couple of days. Do you think you could make them hurry up, Glen?"

"I could give them a call," he promised.

"Is it true that you personally caught the guy?"

"I did, yeah. Though technically it was Harley."

"Harley caught the crook! Oh, that's just fantastic. You didn't get the thing on video, did you? I would love to show it to all of my friends at the senior center."

"No, I didn't get it on video," he said as he caught Poppy's wide grin.

"Too bad. Next time you should. You might become a mean."

"Don't you mean a meme?"

"Yeah, whatever. Anyway, don't forget to call that bank manager and tell him to get off his lazy ass and get me my money back ASAP!"

"I will call your bank manager," he said, more and more starting to feel like his aunt's personal assistant. But then that's what you got with being a cop in the family: everyone came to you with their little—or big—problems to try and solve for them.

"Okay, and now I want you to tell me everything you know about Leah and the baby."

He must have gotten a pained look on his face, for at that moment Poppy took pity on her dear old dad and took over the phone. "What do you want to know, Auntie Lori?"

"Everything! Is it a boy or a girl? Have they picked a name yet? And most importantly: how in the hell did Leah manage to get pregnant at her age!"

CHAPTER 9

They walked into the office, and Holt aimed his coat at the coatrack, missing it by a mile and thus earning himself a grin from Georgina. It was adorable, though, that the old man was trying, she thought. They hadn't told him yet, but the entire team was incredibly grateful that he'd put in a good word with the top brass and managed to score them a considerable promotion by getting them transferred to the Federal Police. Of course, it meant they needed to find suitable lodgings, but that problem had been dealt with—for now. Even Rasheed seemed to enjoy their new setup. Though she still felt he spent way too much time on that gaming console of his—or whatever those things were called. Switch or Twitch or something. Then again, if it didn't interfere with the job and made him happy, why not?

"Okay, I think you're going to want to hear this, boss," said the brainy officer now. "Rumor on the street has it that The Atlas had something to do with the kidnapping of Doctor McMinn."

"Who's The Atlas?" asked Poppy.

"More importantly, when you say 'word on the street,' you probably mean word on Twitch, right?" asked Leland.

"Haha," said Rasheed. "Hilarious, Leland."

"Okay, so who's this Atlas?" Poppy repeated her question as she took a seat on the edge of Rasheed's desk. "Is that even his real name?"

"No, it's not," said Holt. "The Atlas earned his nickname because one side of his face looks like, well, an atlas."

"It's a port-wine stain he's had since he was a kid," said Rasheed. "It covers the left side of his face and looks like a map of the world. He doesn't like the nickname, though."

"Rumor has it that the only person who ever called him The Atlas to his face ended up at the bottom of the Coupure Canal," said Holt.

"His real name is Ari Toropainen," said Rasheed, reading from the man's file. "And if he's behind this kidnapping, that's bad news for Doctor McMinn."

"McMinn is a plastic surgeon, right?" said Georgina. "So maybe The Atlas got sick of his port-wine stain and decided to get rid of it once and for all by engaging McMinn's services?"

"It's possible," Holt admitted. "Better check The Atlas's whereabouts. And then let's pay him a visit. Oh, and while you're at it, Poppy—can you check the story of McMinn being friends with the mental hospital's director and conspiring to have his wife admitted? If it's true, we need to get her out of there."

"Wait, McMinn had his wife committed?" asked Georgina. "That's sick, man."

"She wanted to divorce him, so he had her committed," said Poppy. "At least according to her sister. Not sure if it's true."

"Well, find out," Holt suggested. "It might be the reason he was abducted. Though frankly, I don't really see how his sister-in-law and her husband could be behind it. At least if it's true that the kidnapping looked like the work of a professional crew. As the owners of a daycare center, that kind of thing isn't exactly within the couple's area of expertise."

"They might have friends who do have the know-how," Poppy suggested.

When Holt headed to his desk, Georgina turned her chair around. Across from her, Leland was studying something on his computer, but when she hissed, "Leland!" he looked up. She beckoned him over, and he hurried to join her. "I need your assistance," she said, making sure they weren't overheard. Rasheed was working diligently at his own desk, and Poppy occupied the desk across from her dad, so they were safe.

"Of course," said Leland eagerly, like the good little puppy that he was. "What do you need?"

"How do you feel about a surveillance operation? Like tonight?"

"A surveillance? You mean…"

"The Marquee. I promised Jeanine that I would figure out who spiked her drink. And from talking to her, we determined that it could only have happened at the Marquee."

Last night, when the police had finally arrived on the scene, she had talked to the officer in charge and had discovered what she had already surmised: that Jeanine's incident wasn't an isolated event but part of a bigger problem. Over the last couple of months, easily a dozen girls had come forward claiming to have been spiked. Some of them had also been raped, so things were getting out of hand. A task force had been formed at the local police level, and they were trying to get to the bottom of this business.

"Shouldn't we tell Holt?" Leland whispered.

"No, we shouldn't," she said emphatically.

She had talked to their boss about it, and he had specifically told her that it wasn't their case and they shouldn't step on the local police's toes by interfering. And besides, they had their own investigation to run.

"This would be strictly a private initiative," she said. "Not as police officers, but as concerned citizens. And friends of Jeanine."

Leland nodded. He knew how worried she was about her friend. "Okay, so what do you suggest?"

"I suggest that we go undercover and try to find out what's going on. Maybe we can even draw this guy out by having our own drink spiked."

"You mean: you'd draw this guy out by having *your* drink spiked." He shook his head. "I'm not sure this is a good idea."

"Do you have a better one?"

"Leave it to the task force?"

"They've been investigating this thing for months and haven't made a single arrest. I'd say the task force isn't up to the task. So why don't we give them a helping hand and maybe we'll get lucky." Or unlucky, if this guy managed to spike her drink. Which is why she needed Leland to keep an eye on things. If this guy did spike her drink, he needed to catch him.

"I still don't think it's a good idea. But I can see why you're doing this. So I'm in."

She gave him a dazzling smile that knocked him off his socks. She would have given him a big smacking kiss but knew that would probably give him ideas. Plus, it might put him out of commission for a couple of hours, and she needed him focused and alert for tonight.

"Okay, so Mission Marquee is a go," she said.

"What are you two whispering about?" asked Holt. "It better be about the case."

"Oh, it is about the case, boss," said Leland as he directed a fat wink at Georgina.

CHAPTER 10

Since it was a plausible theory that The Atlas had kidnapped Doctor McMinn to have his face rebuilt, Holt had decided to stake out the clinic where the doctor worked. The Atlas might show up there with the doctor in tow. And since it was customary to organize a stake-out with a partner, he had selected Poppy to join him.

They had parked across the street from the clinic and kept a close eye on the facility to make sure they didn't miss The Atlas coming or going.

"Isn't there a back entrance?" asked Poppy as she dug into a bag of French fries she had picked up from the friterie around the corner. "These are pretty good. Want one?"

He probably should have said yes when she suggested she get him a bag. He picked a particularly fat fry from the heap and had to admit it was pretty tasty. "No back entrance," he said. "I checked." He picked another French fry and dipped it in the glob of mayonnaise.

Poppy watched him with an amused look on her face. "If you want me to get you a bag, just say so, Dad."

"No, it's fine," he said. "I already ate, so I really shouldn't."

"I didn't eat," she explained. When he gave her a curious look, she elaborated, "As you know, I'm not much of a cook, and as I discovered, neither is Bernard. The only thing he knows how to make is Miracoli spaghetti. And even then, he lets the pasta cook too long, turning it soggy. I mean, how can you screw up Miracoli? I don't get it. Even I can do it!"

Holt had tasted his daughter's pasta and would have argued that she, too, was one of the rare people who managed to mess up the Miracoli pasta classics. But he wasn't going to tell her that. Bad as her cooking was, he still missed it. It wasn't a lot of fun living alone—even though he had Harley to keep him company. As he was keeping them company now, seated in the backseat and looking far too happy to be on a stake-out with them.

"You know, we really have to get that poor woman out of that mental institution," said Poppy as she stuffed a couple more fries into her mouth. "I mean, that's just an awful, awful thing that doctor did. For that reason alone, he deserves to suffer a terrible fate at the hands of this Atlas guy."

"Nobody deserves to be kidnapped, Poppy," he said. Though he could see what she meant. If the well-renowned plastic surgeon really had manipulated his friendship with the institution's director to get his wife committed so he could get custody of his son, that was a terrible thing to do. "Have you found out if what the sister told us is true?"

She nodded vigorously, but it took a while until she had cleared away those fries before she could talk. "I did, yeah. Turns out she was right. McMinn did go to medical school with both Judson Singh and Shawn Luukkonen. They were best friends all through college and still are to this day. Though when I talked to Doctor Singh on the phone, he was extremely evasive."

"You should threaten him with a complaint to the Order

of Physicians. Maybe he'll be more amenable to conversation."

"Great idea, Dad," she said. "I'll do that then. And I'll also talk to this Luukkonen fellow. See what he has to say for himself. I mean, if any doctor can get his wife committed to a mental hospital... I mean, that's just..." She struggled to find the right words. "That's just... mean!"

Mean was quite the understatement.

He glanced at that bag of fries again and decided to have one last one. They shouldn't be so good. But when he tried to pick one, Poppy slapped his hand away. "Not good for your waistline, Dad. If you ever wanted to start dating again, you need to make sure you stay in good shape."

"I'm not going to start dating again," he said, and made another attempt to snag a fry.

"Well, you should," she said as she thwarted his second attempt with remarkable skill and determination. "You're still young, Dad. You can find love again, and you should."

"Like your mom did, you mean?"

She gave him a look of concern, the same look she had been directing at him ever since the day he had aimed a well-placed right hook at his former boss's jaw when he came upon him and Leah engaging in carnal relations on his boss's desk.

"You have to move on, Dad. And look, I know it's hard. Especially now that Mom is having another baby."

"That's got nothing to do with me," he said emphatically.

"See? That's exactly what I mean," she said. "You're suffering, Dad. Living in the past. Even now you can't get over the fact that it's over and that Mom has moved on."

"Oh, I'm over it," he assured her. "I have moved on."

"Oh, Dad," she said as she patted him on the arm.

He gritted his teeth. Why did everyone treat him like a victim to feel pity for? Even if Leah hadn't had the affair, he had known in his heart of hearts that the marriage had run its course and that they were basically living parallel lives.

He hadn't even been all that upset when he discovered her having an affair with his boss. Even though he had still felt the need to punch the man's lights out. He didn't understand where that had come from. Leah had told him that he was a brute, had always been a brute, and this was the evidence.

He didn't think he necessarily was a brute, though. He had asked Poppy, and she had laughed so hard he felt a little insulted. He might not be a brute, but he liked to think he was a man's man. But when he said that, she had laughed even harder. Okay, so maybe the image he had formed of himself wasn't exactly in line with reality. All he knew was that it had felt pretty good to punch his boss in the face. Too good, in fact. Which might point to unresolved rage issues, like Leah claimed.

He'd spent a couple of weeks frequenting a shrink. Not because he wanted to, but because his bosses had ordered him to while they tried to figure out what to do with him. The shrink had told him that he may have felt emasculated by his boss, though he failed to understand quite what that might entail.

Just then, his phone chimed, and he glanced at the display. "It's Leland." He picked up. "Leland?"

"Boss? Can you come? It's Georgina. Someone spiked her drink."

CHAPTER 11

Georgina was getting antsy. They'd been at the club for hours and nothing was happening. She was a can-do kind of girl, and all this sitting around waiting wasn't her thing. She had made sure to leave her drink unattended several times, hoping the spiker would seize his opportunity, but so far no dice.

She made eye contact with Leland, who was strategically located at the far side of the bar, making sure not to draw attention to himself, but he shook his head. Nothing doing.

Christ. She was starting to wonder if maybe this spiker had a certain type, and she wasn't it. Or he simply wasn't there tonight. They really should get access to the investigation to find out if he had certain days he struck and if he always targeted the same type of women. Her friend Jeanine was dark-haired, though, and so was she. Though it had to be said that Jeanine was a lot slimmer than she was. Petite, she liked to describe herself. You could say a lot of things about Georgina, but she definitely was not petite.

She glanced in the direction of the dance floor, which was already thinning out, with only the regulars still going strong and trying to go the long haul and stick around until dawn. And since they had to work tomorrow, she figured they should call it a night. So she downed the remainder of her drink and slipped off her bar stool. As she did, she experienced a sudden weakening at the knees, as if she'd had too much to drink.

As she tried to regain her balance, suddenly the room was spinning, and if a helping arm hadn't supported her, she would have hit the deck—face-planting in front of all of these people. Oh, the horror.

She gratefully allowed her chivalrous knight to escort her to the door. Which is when it hit her that maybe this was it. Maybe this was what it felt like to be drugged!

But as she staggered on, supported by whoever was assisting her, her field of vision started to narrow more and more, darkness moving in from every side, and before long, she lost control of her limbs and sagged against the person.

She managed to glance up at whoever it was that was dragging her along and saw that he was a young man with incredibly good looks. But as her eyes drooped closed, she was vaguely aware of some kind of altercation that erupted close by. The next moment, she was tumbling deeper and deeper into the abyss.

* * *

LELAND ALMOST MISSED the whole thing. One moment he had been watching Georgina, and the next a pretty girl approached him, and he couldn't help but be distracted when she gave him a dazzling smile. He was on the verge of introducing himself when he became aware of Georgina being led away by a man he hadn't noticed before. He was shocked to see that his colleague had trouble walking and was leaning heavily against this mystery man.

As he slipped off his bar stool and headed in her direction, he was momentarily waylaid by the pretty girl, who was holding two drinks and offering him one. Under different circumstances, he would happily have taken her up on the offer, but not now. And so he made a helpless motion and slipped past her. By the time he caught up with Georgina, she was already outside, practically being dragged along by that man. And as he realized that this must be the spiker, a sudden burst of rage built up inside him to such a degree that he practically pummeled the guy in the back the moment he reached the pair.

The guy looked up, deeply surprised, and when he found himself face to face with a furious Leland, he must have understood that the gig was up. He immediately shoved Georgina in Leland's direction and broke into a run.

For a moment, Leland wavered: should he go after the guy or stay with Georgina and make sure she was all right? Lucky for him, one of the bouncers showed up at that exact moment, and so he pointed to the unconscious figure of his colleague on the ground. "Call an ambulance! Somebody drugged her!"

And then he burst into a sprint, chasing after the culprit.

The guy had a head start and was going strong in the direction of the Muinkschelde Canal. But Leland wasn't a slouch in the running department either, and he managed to keep up well and even gain on the guy. He wasn't helped by the fact that they were in an area where the streetlights weren't exactly omnipresent, and certain sections were almost plunged into darkness. He could still see the guy from time to time as his feet slapped the sidewalk, running full tilt now.

They'd reached the canal, and the spiker turned left, which would take him to the old Saint Peter's Abbey. Leland pumped his arms as he tried to figure out a way of cutting the guy off before he reached Saint Peter's Square and disappeared into the maze of streets beyond. But as he turned a corner, there was no sight of the guy. He had vanished!

Christ! He kept on running, but it was no use. Somehow Georgina's attacker had managed to get away from him. And since he was more worried about his friend and colleague by now than combing through every single street to find the guy, he started retracing his steps back to the Marquee, hoping his partner would be all right.

As he did, he took out his phone and dialed the familiar number. When he told Holt what happened, it was safe to say he was less than impressed by his sorry tale of woe.

CHAPTER 12

$\mathcal{H}$olt was furious. But more than that, he was deeply concerned about Georgina. When he and Poppy arrived on the scene, Leland had just returned from trying to catch the guy responsible for spiking their colleague. When they reached the stricken inspector, the sight of her pale face caused Holt to wish he could put his hands around the culprit's throat and squeeze—hard.

Poppy immediately sank down next to Georgina, but it was clear she was completely unresponsive. Whatever they had done to her had been pretty effective. The bouncer Leland had left in charge of the situation had carefully placed Georgina on a blanket on the ground and had been guarding her closely, even as he was in touch with the first aid people.

"The ambulance should be here shortly," he announced. With his face tattoos and bald head, he might look like a villain from one of the Lord of the Rings movies, but it was clear that he had his heart in the right place.

Holt nodded curtly. "Who did this?" he asked.

Leland shrugged. "I've never seen him before. Handsome

young man—probably in his early twenties. Looked like he could be a student. Fast, too. I lost him near the canal."

"Did you see him?" he asked the bouncer.

The guy shook his head. "I'm sorry, but I was dealing with something inside when it happened. By the time I came out, your friend was on the ground, and this guy asked me to call an ambulance, which is what I did."

"Christ, what were you two doing here in the first place?" asked Holt. "This isn't one of your regular haunts, is it?" Mostly, the Marquee was known as a techno club, and as far as he knew, neither Leland nor Georgina were part of that scene.

"We were trying to stage a trap," said Leland, looking extremely uncomfortable now.

"You were what?!" he spat.

"One of Georgina's friends was spiked yesterday," the young inspector explained, his eyes not quite meeting Holt's. "And so Georgina figured that we should try and catch this guy in the act, seeing as the task force isn't exactly making a lot of progress. And so she left her drink unattended while I kept a close eye on it from the other side of the bar."

Holt tamped down on the irritation he felt that his two officers had decided to launch this impromptu and unsanctioned operation—putting themselves at serious risk.

"Okay, so you were seated on one end of the bar, and Georgina was on the other end. And you kept a close eye on her drink at all times. So how did it get spiked?"

Leland swallowed with difficulty. "I guess... I must have gotten distracted at some point."

Holt would have read him the riot act, but now wasn't the time or the place. Leland looked upset enough as it was, and the ambulance still hadn't shown up.

"How is she?" he asked Poppy.

His daughter shook her head. "Still unresponsive."

"This guy really did a number on her," said Holt. He glanced over to the bouncer. "Do you operate CCTV in this club?"

"No, we don't," he said, which wasn't a big surprise. A lot of these clubs turned a blind eye when their clubbers enjoyed a hit of whatever floated their boat. Pills of every color and description were freely distributed in these types of clubs. No owner would incriminate himself by operating a CCTV camera system to catch all of that on film for the police to see.

"Let's talk to the bartender," said Holt. "See if he can't tell us what happened. You stay here with Georgina until the ambulance arrives," he told his daughter. "You're with me," he added for Leland's benefit.

Together the two men strode into the club. When they arrived at the bar, Holt saw that the bartender was a heavily tattooed man with plenty of piercings. He'd half expected to see his daughter's boyfriend Bernard, but if he remembered correctly, he worked at a different club. "Can we talk?" he yelled over the din of the music, flashing his badge in the guy's face.

The bartender pointed to the exit, then asked one of the other people behind the bar to take over for a moment, and followed Holt and Leland outside. He seemed genuinely surprised to see an unconscious Georgina lying on the ground.

"What happened?" he asked.

"She was spiked," Holt said curtly.

"Did you see who did this?" asked Leland.

The man, whose name was Balto Sliz, frowned as he took in the disconcerting scene. "I'm sorry, no. I did see your friend at the bar, but I didn't notice anything out of the ordinary." He clucked his tongue. "This is bad. Yesterday a girl was spiked, and now another one."

"Is the owner on the premises?" asked Holt.

"No, he's not. He rarely shows his face, to be honest. Mostly it's the manager who takes care of things, like organizing the schedule and making sure that everyone is in position."

"Who's the manager?"

"Sammy Barton. But he left about an hour ago, when he was sure that everyone was here and things were running smoothly."

"And you didn't see a young man put something in Georgina's drink?" asked Holt. "Describe him, Leland."

"Um, well, he was probably in his early twenties," said Leland as he scratched his neck. "Handsome. Blond curly hair. He wore jeans and a, um, red shirt and white sneakers. Fast runner, so he might be into sports."

"Rings a bell?" asked Holt.

But Balto shook his head. "Can't say that it does. But then I'm usually so busy mixing drinks that I don't really pay a lot of attention to what happens on the floor."

"But you did notice Georgina."

"Yes, but that's because she's a regular."

"Okay, thanks," said Holt. "You'll have to repeat what you just said to my colleagues."

"A specialist task force has been set up to track down this spiker," Leland explained. "But it's not us—it's other officers."

"Of course," said Balto. "Whatever you need to catch this guy. I know other clubs have been forced to close because of dirtbags like him, so I want him caught as much as you do."

Holt nodded curtly and watched the bartender head in.

"God, what's taking this ambulance so long?" Leland groaned. He glanced down at Georgina. "If only I hadn't agreed to her idea of trying to catch this guy. Or if I had kept a closer eye on her drink. Only I kept getting distracted by this girl, you know."

Holt's head snapped up. "What girl?"

"Oh, just some girl. She popped up around the time Georgina's glass must have been spiked. Hovered around me for a while and even offered me a drink." As understanding dawned, his jaw dropped. "You don't think…"

Holt's own jaw worked. "It could be a coincidence, of course. Or it's also possible that the spiker, whoever he is, clocked your presence and decided to enlist the assistance of this girl to distract you so he could do his business undetected." He nodded. "You better get in there, son, and try to locate this girl."

Leland hurried inside again, only to return about ten minutes later, shaking his head. "She must have left."

"Of course she did," said Holt. Which told him that his hunch just might be correct and that, for whatever reason, she was working with the rapist.

At that moment, the ambulance finally arrived, and Georgina got the medical assistance she required. A brief examination told them that she wouldn't suffer any long-term effects, but just to be on the safe side, they decided to take her to the hospital where they could keep an eye on her.

Leland offered to ride in the ambulance with their colleague, and Poppy and Holt watched as the paramedics placed Georgina on a stretcher, then into the ambulance, and took off.

"This is turning into quite the eventful night," said Poppy.

"You can say that again."

"Too bad we didn't catch The Atlas in the act of sneaking into McMinn's clinic."

When the call came in from Leland, he had asked a couple of officers to sit on the clinic, just to make sure The Atlas didn't show up. But he hadn't heard back from them, so it was safe to say that his hunch wasn't going to play out. At least not tonight.

It wasn't long before members of the task force showed up, and he and Poppy gave their account of the night's events. They'd interview the manager and staff members in the morning. Georgina and Leland would also have to give their statements, and hopefully they'd be able to work with the description Leland had given to nab the guy and put a stop to his activities once and for all.

So in a sense, Leland and Georgina had done good. At least they'd been proactive, which was more than could be said about this so-called task force.

But that didn't mean he wasn't going to give them hell. But only when Georgina was back on her feet and recovered from her terrible ordeal.

He couldn't deny he was proud of his officers, though. But he wasn't going to tell them that. First, he'd let them stew.

CHAPTER 13

Barney Waller was one of those lucky souls who got to live on a canal barge on one of the many canals that crisscross Ghent. Barney had been living on his barge long before it became fashionable or cool to do so, back when it was more a sign of poverty and not being able to afford the exorbitant rental prices. Though, in all honesty, it had been circumstances that had pushed him into selecting a canal boat to live on rather than a conscious choice.

After his wife had died, he'd found his life slowly spiraling out of control. Maybelle had been the force that kept their shared lives balanced and worth living for. Once she was gone, he just couldn't be bothered and, in short order, had lost his job, his domicile, and all of his friends. Even his kids had broken all ties with him, and he had ended up living on the street for a while. Until he struck up a friendship with Grady, a fellow homeless person, who discovered this deserted and derelict boat, tucked away in a remote part of Ghent's canal system, and had selected it as a refuge for the cold winter nights.

Barney had joined the old man, and together they had fixed the boat up as well as they could with the limited skills and materials they possessed. Barney had christened it The Maybelle, after his late wife, and the canal barge had become their little secret until the town council decided to organize a big clean-up and get rid of all of these old wrecks by towing them away and dismantling them.

When it came time for Barney and Grady's boat to suffer the same fate, some of the neighborhood people organized a campaign to have the boat restored to its former glory and for the two homeless men to officially take possession of the canal barge.

Before long, the town decided to honor the neighborhood's request, and Barney and Grady had been officially registered as owners of the old barge, which had been towed from its location to the Coupure Canal, where it had been moored for the past fifteen years. Grady had passed away a couple of winters ago, and now it was just Barney.

With his long unkempt white hair and beard, he was a recognizable figure in the neighborhood, and even though he was officially not homeless anymore, he still acted as if he was, taking his begging bowl to the local supermarket to pick up some extra change, even though the town had arranged a pension and benefits so he didn't lack for anything.

He'd been fast asleep when he woke up from the sound of a splash. And when he peered through the porthole, he saw that something had been thrown into the water. Next to him, another boat lay moored, and as he glanced over, he saw that a pair of keen eyes stared right back at him. He immediately retreated from the window. Long years of living rough had taught him never to get involved in anyone else's business lest it cause trouble for him.

Too bad he had recognized the person in the next barge.

It meant that the person might also have recognized him.

* * *

A LIGHT FOG had settled over the canal, as it often did early in the morning, but that didn't dissuade the habitual fishermen from casting out their lines in the hope of catching something they could boast about to their fellow hobbyists. Some of them kept their catch, but strictly speaking, this was forbidden, as caught fish had to be immediately thrown back in. It wasn't about supplementing your diet on the cheap but all about the sport.

The Coupure Canal was by far the most popular spot for amateur fishermen to throw out their lines. You could find carp there, bream, and pike-perch—not exactly small fry. One of those avid fishers was Freddy Risto, who had been coming there for years. Once upon a time, there wasn't a lot of fish in these canals, as the water was too polluted. But measures had been taken over the years, gradually the fish had returned, and so had the fishermen.

Freddy, whose favorite spot was beyond the Groenevallei Park, sat on his stool rolling a cigarette while keeping one eye on his line when all of a sudden he thought he saw something floating on the water. As he looked closer, he frowned.

"Hey, Jim!" he yelled to his buddy.

"Shush!" Jim yelled back. "You'll scare the fish with your noise!"

"What's that thing over there?"

Jim joined him, and both stood on the shore staring at the object that floated past. Just then, a fish must have decided to take an interest in the object. The movement of the fish made the object turn over in the water, and suddenly a hand appeared.

Both Freddy and Jim uttered an involuntary cry.

"It's a person!" Freddy said.

Jim was already taking his phone from his pocket and calling the emergency services.

Meanwhile, Freddy had grabbed hold of his hook and tried to get the corpse to the shore. After a couple of tries, he finally succeeded. In the process, the body had flipped around, and both men now found themselves staring down at the face of a woman.

If they had wondered whether they should try to jump in to save her, the lifeless eyes staring back at them, combined with the deep cuts to the throat the woman had suffered, were enough to dissuade them from such a pointless endeavor.

"Looks like she's dead," said Freddy soberly.

"Yes, a woman in the water," Jim spoke into his phone. "She's dead."

Freddy frowned. "Hey, wait a minute. I think I know her. Isn't that the dentist from down the road?" He was pointing upstream. "What's her name again?" Then he snapped his fingers. "Kirkpatrick! Dentist Kirkpatrick!"

"We think her name is Kirkpatrick," Jim spoke into the phone. He hung up. "They'll be here soon," he said.

For a moment, he and Freddy simply stared down at the poor woman.

"She must have accidentally fallen in," Jim determined.

"Then how do you explain those marks on her throat? No fish did that, Jim."

"Maybe she cut herself going in? There are boats here, you know."

"Only kayaks," said Freddy.

"Oh, and what do you call that?" asked Jim, and pointed to a small pleasure boat that was puttering away along the canal. They were the kind of boats that could be rented and took tourists all through the intricate Ghent canal system.

71

"She must have fallen in, and drowned, and then got chopped up by one of them boats."

"Imagine that," said Freddy with a shiver.

He still couldn't quite see it. But then again, he was no cop.

CHAPTER 14

It had been a short night, what with the stake-out at the McMinn clinic and Georgina getting spiked, but that didn't stop Poppy from being first to arrive at the scene where the woman had been found floating in the water. It helped that she was living close by, and so were Georgina, Leland, and Rasheed, who arrived within five minutes of her.

It took Holt longer, but then he had to drive all the way from Loveringem, which usually took about half an hour, but now with rush hour was closer to forty-five minutes. And even then, he had to contend with all the cyclists, who descended on the Coupure in droves. The entire length of the street lining the canal had been turned into a so-called cycling street, where cyclists ruled and cars had to adapt their speed. Not today, though, for this section of the canal had been cordoned off so the police and the CSI team could do their jobs.

"A dentist?" she asked. "Are you sure?"

The police officer who had been first on the scene

pointed to two old guys standing nearby. Judging from their outfits, they were probably amateur fishermen. "According to these gentlemen, her name is Kirkpatrick and she lives on Coupure Rechts closer to the Saint Agnete Bridge, in a very fancy house. Their words, not mine," he stressed with a grin.

Georgina, Leland, and Rasheed came hurrying up, and Poppy eyed her colleague with concern. "You shouldn't be here," she told Georgina. "You should be home resting."

"I'd rather be torn limb from limb than to stay home when I'm feeling perfectly fine," said Georgina in her usual forceful way. "I'm fine!" she repeated. "I feel great."

"You didn't look so great last night."

"So I passed out," she said with a shrug. "Could happen to anyone. You should have seen me back in the day when I was still clubbing full-time. I passed out more than once."

"But not from being spiked by a rapist."

Georgina's eyes clouded, telling Poppy that she was aware of the close escape she'd had. "Okay, so what do we have here?" said Georgina as she donned a pair of plastic gloves, even though it wasn't strictly necessary. They weren't going to pull the body out of the water. A team of divers would.

"According to those two gentlemen over there, she's a dentist," said Poppy. "Lives down the road in a fancy house."

"Dentists do make a lot of money," Leland said. "Well, more than we do, at least," he amended his statement when Rasheed gave him a strange look. His parents were dentists.

Holt's car now came driving up and parked on what was normally the busiest bicycling street in town but was now fully devoid of cyclists. He hurried out of his vehicle, and Poppy noticed how he must have cut himself shaving, for he had stuck a band-aid to his cheek and then forgot about it. She gestured to her cheek and he quickly removed the band-aid.

"Georgina?" he said as he gave her a nod. "Shouldn't you be—"

"No!" she cried. Then she seemed to remember who she was talking to, and seeing Holt's surprised look, said in a calmer tone, "I'm fine, sir. Perfectly fit for duty."

"Okay," he said, holding up his hands in a defensive gesture. "So who's the victim?"

"Dentist, sir," said Leland.

"Accidental drowning?" he asked. But then shook his head. "If it was, we wouldn't have been called out here. So I'm guessing this was murder."

He descended down the bank as far as he could go without falling into the water, crouched down, and studied the body, which was being kept from floating away with a fish hook for some reason. "Those marks on her neck," he said as Poppy approached. "Does that look like stab wounds to you?"

She crouched down next to her dad. "I would say so," she admitted.

"So stabbed in the throat and thrown into the water," he said, nodding. "I'm guessing she hasn't been in the water long, from the condition of the body. Though we better leave those determinations up to Tomas." He stared in the direction of the Saint Agnete Bridge. "She must have floated down here from that direction, considering the stream, so it's safe to say we'll find our crime scene somewhere along the bank —either right or left."

"According to the first officer on the scene, she lives on Coupure Rechts."

"So the right side of the canal." He glanced down at the body. "She's dressed in running clothes, so could be she was out running when she was attacked. Which would make sense as this path is popular with joggers." He climbed back up the bank of the canal, with Poppy following his lead.

She couldn't imagine being attacked while going for a run and being dumped into the canal. And to think this was generally considered a safe neighborhood. Once upon a time, the Coupure was where all the rich people lived, with poorer ones not even allowed access, and even to this day the houses lining the canal were some of the posher ones in town.

"Okay, you better gather a team and search the bank of the canal," Holt told the rest of the team. "We need to find the crime scene. There will probably be plenty of blood, as she may have been stabbed to death while she was out jogging."

"What do you want me to do?" asked Poppy as Leland, Georgina, and Rasheed left to liaise with the local police to organize a search of the bank of the canal.

"We're going to wait until those divers get that poor woman out of the canal and Tomas can make a first determination. Then we'll pay a visit to the woman's family to give them the bad news and try and start reconstructing her final hours."

He glanced upstream at a couple of canal barges moored there. "We better organize a neighborhood canvass. Go door to door to see if anyone saw anything." He pointed at the barges. "And that includes the people living on those canal boats over there."

She made a mental note of this and looked up when the van with the divers arrived, followed by another van carrying the coroner's team. Tomas Lovelass wasted no time heading down to where they were waiting. As usual, he looked as if he'd just returned from a funeral, a dark frown on his face and bags under his eyes. But then when you dealt with death all day, every day, you probably started to look the way he did. Like an undertaker.

"Let's get her out of there," he said after he had surveyed the scene.

Two divers went into the water, and it wasn't long before

they had managed to lift the woman out of the canal and onto the bank. All along the Coupure, a concrete border had been constructed in the early eighties, and it made getting in and out of the water practically impossible. Meanwhile, a couple of ducks surveyed the scene from a safe distance, probably wondering what was going on and what these strange big birds were up to.

Once the body of the woman had been brought up to the path that ran along the canal, Tomas got to work, impatiently watched by Holt.

"And?" he asked finally when he ran out of patience. "How did she die, doc?"

"Stabbed in the throat, I would think. Probably dead by the time her body hit the water."

"Time of death?"

"No sooner than twenty-four hours, no later than twelve." When Holt groaned, he gave him a look of annoyance. "That's the best I can do for now, Holt. She's been in the water, which makes it difficult to determine the exact time of death. But then you know that as well as I do," he added as he got up.

"So stabbed between yesterday morning and yesterday evening," said Holt, summing things up succinctly. "Anything else you can tell me?"

Tomas was studying the woman's fingernails. "I don't see signs of a struggle," he said. "So the attack took her by surprise." He let his gaze slide down her body. "Jogging outfit, I'd say. Considering the location, it's possible she was out running when she was attacked."

Which had been Holt's conclusion also, but then Poppy's dad rarely missed a trick.

"I knew her, you know," suddenly Tomas said. "She was a dentist, and a good one."

"Was she your dentist?" asked Holt.

Tomas permitted himself a rare smile. "Unfortunately, no. She specialized in orthodontic dentistry. We shared a few courses in our first bachelor year but lost touch after that." He sighed deeply. "She was lovely. Just lovely."

Holt and Poppy shared a look. "You used to date?" asked Holt, never afraid to ask the tough or embarrassing questions.

Tomas frowned. "Of course we didn't *date*. We were friendly, that's all."

"Does that mean you don't know Mr. Kirkpatrick?"

"Oh, I know Sebastian," said Tomas in measured tones. "Or at least I know of him."

Holt waited to see if he'd say more, but the coroner seemed to have exhausted the topic. He raised his mournful gaze to meet Holt's. "If you'll excuse me, I have to arrange for Margo's body to be taken to the morgue."

"Okay, thanks Tomas," said Holt, and turned away from the grisly scene. "Let's go talk to Mr. Kirkpatrick," he suggested. "And find out what kind of person lovely Margo was."

Just then, Holt's phone buzzed in his pocket. When he took it out, he stared at the display with an exasperated look on his face. Knowing her dad, Poppy knew there was only one person in the world who could elicit this look.

"Leah?" he said curtly. He listened for a moment, his frown deepening. "I'm in the middle of something right now. Can't we do this later?" When she simply kept on talking, as she usually did, a vein started pulsating in his right temple. "Not now!" he grunted, and promptly hung up. He stood there for a moment, until he became aware of his daughter's presence. "She wanted to talk. About the baby. I told her not now."

"Yeah, I heard," she said, unsuccessfully hiding her smile.

"God, that woman," he growled, and legged it back to his car. Poppy followed him, wondering not for the first time how her parents had managed to stay married as long as they had.

CHAPTER 15

*D*elivering a death message was probably the least favorite task any police officer could be asked to attend to. But since it had to be done, Holt had decided a long time ago not to dwell on it but simply get it over with, with as much empathy as he could muster. Which was something he'd had to learn, since showing empathy didn't come naturally to him.

It did to Poppy, though. In spades. In fact, his daughter had so much empathy it sometimes impeded other tasks, such as getting information out of the relatives about the victim.

And so Poppy had been holding Mr. Kirkpatrick's hand for the past five minutes while the man wept bitter tears, while Holt studied their surroundings. The room they were in was spacious and very light and bright. Located on the second floor of what could only be a million-euro home, it looked out across the Coupure through the front window and some lovely gardens through the back. A dog was sniffing at Holt's feet and giving him nasty glances—probably unhappy that he was tracking Harley's scent into his territory.

"Lovely pictures," he said as he gestured to one of many portraits of what he could only assume was Mrs. Kirkpatrick.

The husband of the deceased looked up and wiped his eyes. "Yeah, we're very proud of her success. My club was where she got her big break, you know. But then of course everyone knows the story by now. She's told it in every single interview."

Holt was confused. "I thought your wife was a dentist?"

"That's not Mrs. Kirkpatrick, sir," said Poppy. "That's Ruby Floss."

The name rang a bell. "Floss?"

"The singer?" said Poppy as she resisted the urge to roll her eyes. The way she always did when she figured her dad was being obtuse. *"Mark my Spot?"*

"What spot?" he asked.

"It's Ruby's biggest hit," Kirkpatrick explained. "Platinum in thirty different countries. Made her an overnight star. Did you know the song was actually recorded in my studio?"

"You have a studio?" asked Poppy. She had settled back on the cream-colored couch now, her hand-holding services no longer required.

"Well, I did," said the man as he pressed a tissue paper to his eyes. His face looked suspiciously wrinkle-free, Holt thought, and his hair very dark. "Back in the day, all the big acts recorded at my place. But then when my clubs started taking off big time, I didn't have the time anymore. And also, standards were raised and I couldn't keep up. But I launched that girl's career," he said as he pointed to one of the pictures on the wall. It depicted a young lady dressed in an electric pink leotard, fresh-faced and eager to impress.

"So when did you last see your wife?" asked Holt, not all that interested in the world of pop music.

"Um… must have been before I left last night," he said. "Around ten, maybe?"

"And you left to go… where, exactly?"

"The Pussycat. One of my clubs. I own several. Though I spend most of my time at the Pussycat, since it's my newest addition and I'm trying to make it take off. The others are more established."

"And when you returned home, you didn't see her?"

"By the time I got home I figured she'd already gone to bed. This must have been around three or four last night." He gave them a smile. "I'm a night owl. Always have been. It helps if you own a string of nightclubs. My wife knew this about me, and she was fine with it. We usually had breakfast together, though, and then afterwards I went back to bed until mid-afternoon. Only this morning she didn't wake me, so I slept until you woke me up."

"You didn't notice that she was gone?" asked Holt.

"Well, no. Since I got back so late, I slept in the second bedroom. Margo has always been a light sleeper, and she hated it when I got into bed and woke her up. So we came up with this arrangement, and it benefited us both. She got a good night's sleep, and I didn't have to worry about arriving home in the middle of the night—which I only did because this is my business," he hastened to add, lest they got the wrong idea.

"She was dressed in a jogging outfit," said Poppy. "Do you think she went for a run?"

"Margo was into sports and fitness big time. She had a subscription at this gym across the street and spent a lot of time there. And when she wasn't at the gym she went running."

"Did she run at night or in the morning?"

"Mostly at night," said the man, nodding. Then he started. "You don't think…" He stared at them, wide-eyed. "Are you saying she was attacked while she was out running?"

"At this stage we're ruling nothing out," said Poppy, well-trained in deflection. "But considering she was dressed in her jogging outfit, it's a possibility we can't rule out."

The man rubbed his face. "My God. I told her a million times she shouldn't go running at night. You never know what creeps may be lurking out there." He pressed his eyes closed. "I can just see it now. Margo going for a late-night run, some guy waiting for her behind a tree and snap." He looked up. "How was she…" He gulped. "I mean, how did she…"

"Maybe it's better if you don't know," Poppy said gently.

"That bad, huh?" He gulped a few more times. "Can I see her? I mean, I have to identify her, right? Or is that only in the movies?"

"You can see her," said Holt. "But only if you feel up to it."

The man nodded. "I think I want to see her. To say good-bye, you know. We had been married twenty-five years. A long time to be together. And now all of a sudden… she's… gone." His voice broke and he started weeping again. This time Poppy didn't clutch his hand in hers. Probably because Holt gave her a stern look.

"Had your wife received any threats?" he asked, eager to conclude the interview without too many interruptions. "Or gotten involved in an argument with a patient, maybe?"

The man shook his head. "Margo was an angel. Everyone loved her, and especially her patients adored her. She had specialized in orthodontics, so mostly her patients were kids and teenagers, and they all spoke highly of her. She was extremely good at what she did, you see. But more than that, she was a real mensch—a woman with a heart of gold."

"How about you?" asked Holt.

"What about me?"

"Did you recently get into any entanglements—personal or business—that might have turned you into a target?"

He stared at Holt, eyes wide. "You don't think they're after *me*, do you?"

"It's a possibility we have to explore," he said patiently. "Sometimes when a person is attacked, the perpetrators are in fact trying to send a message. It's just one of many possible lines of inquiry," he hastened to add when the man's face went white as a sheet.

"Well, I don't need to explain to you that the world of nightclubs is pretty brutal. I mean, I have competitors who'd love to see the back of me. Or run my businesses into the ground. But they'd never resort to violence, I don't think. Or target my wife. I mean, that would be unheard of."

"So you haven't received any threats lately?"

"No, I haven't. And I hope you're barking up the wrong tree. Because if it turns out that I'm responsible for what happened to..." His face screwed up and he started sobbing.

This time Poppy ignored her dad and proceeded to rub the man's back. In the end, she held him in her arms and gently rocked him back and forth while Holt inwardly groaned.

CHAPTER 16

"You really should show some sympathy, dad," she said when they finally left. "I mean, the guy just lost his wife, for goodness sakes. Of course he's going to be devastated. Of course he's going to be sad. And then you start bombarding him with a million questions. Even I know that you can't expect a person like that to sit there and not feel crushed."

"There's crushed and crushed," grunted Holt. "All he did was cry the whole time. I mean, what happened to taking it like a man?"

"Dad!"

"If a cop showed up on my doorstep back when I was still married to your mother and told me they just fished her body out of the canal, you wouldn't have seen me falling to pieces like that. Or weeping like a baby. Our generation—"

"Oh, God. Here we go."

"Our generation took it on the chin, honey. That's the difference. We didn't walk around with our hearts on our sleeves. Stiff upper lip, remember?"

"That's a British thing, Dad. We're Belgian."

"It's the same thing."

"Well, I beg to differ. I think it's very healthy to be in touch with your emotions and not to bury them and let them fester."

"At least now we know she was probably attacked last night. Though it seems a little suspicious to me that he didn't even notice that his wife was gone until we arrived."

"He slept in the second bedroom, Dad. He explained all that. Plus, he worked until three or four o'clock last night and only woke up when we got there."

"Says he," he grumbled.

Poppy just couldn't with this man and his stone-age ideas about how to deal with grief. But instead of telling him how she felt—which he wouldn't appreciate—she decided to bite her tongue. Or not. "So when are you going to talk to Mom about the baby?"

"Not again with the baby!" he yelled as he threw up his hands.

"See? You *can* be in touch with your emotions if you want to be."

He gave her a dirty look and she grinned. Holt might be an old fossil from a bygone age, but that didn't mean he was a bad person. She knew he had a good heart. You just had to dig deep to find it. Very, very deep.

They finally arrived at the cars and they each got into their respective vehicles and took off in the direction of the Groendreef, where the Federal Police had its headquarters. She cast her mind back to the interview with Sebastian and wondered how she had never heard the story that he had been Ruby Floss's mentor and producer back in the day. Ruby was a big star now. But like all stars came from humble beginnings, right here in little ol' Ghent.

She wondered if there was a connection between Margo's

death and Ruby Floss but couldn't see how. Clearly, Ruby's days as a fledgling singer lay in the distant past.

As she turned on the radio, through some kind of mysterious happenstance, the song that she had referred to, *Mark my Spot*, came on, and Poppy ended up singing along at the top of her voice. It was the anthem of her generation, the song that had colored her childhood. She even remembered Mom once took her to a Ruby Floss concert, back when Ruby was still primarily a singer for kids and teens. Later, she had moved away from that and become a pop sensation, tackling an older audience and becoming a massive success.

Poppy had plastered Ruby posters all over her bedroom and had driven her parents crazy wanting to go to every appearance, whether it be at the local mall or the market. Until she turned thirteen and some boy band had snagged her attention, and Ruby was forgotten.

Back at the station, she watched as her dad tried to aim his coat at the coatrack and failed. He wasn't giving up, though, and one of these days he'd manage to hit his target.

She shared a look of amusement with Georgina and was glad to see her colleague back on her feet. After last night, she figured they wouldn't see her for weeks. But Georgina was made of sterner stuff and wasn't deterred so easily—not even by a wannabe rapist.

"Have you heard anything from the task force?" she asked.

Georgina shook her head. "Nothing yet. The guy is like a ghost. Seems to be able to disappear into thin air. It's freaky."

"They'll catch him sooner or later," said Leland. "At some point his luck will run out and someone will nail that..." He muttered a few curse words, indicating how he felt about the guy who had targeted their colleague. It elicited a grateful smile from Georgina. If it hadn't been for Leland, who knows what might have happened last night.

"Okay, so this is interesting," said Rasheed. "You'll never guess who Margo Kirkpatrick's brother is."

They all gathered around the technically gifted detective's desk. "Well, don't keep us in suspense," said Holt. "Who?"

Instead of responding, Rasheed pulled up a mugshot on his screen. Poppy stared at a man whose menacing eyes were only the second most scary aspect of his presence. The most noticeable thing was the large wine-port stain that covered half of his face.

"The Atlas," she muttered.

"What are the odds?" said her dad.

"The Atlas is the victim's brother?" asked Georgina.

"Margo Kirkpatrick was born Margo Toropainen," said Rasheed. "But took her husband's name when she got married."

"Her husband neglected to tell us that," said Holt, and he didn't sound happy about it. "Better bring him in, Poppy. We need to have another chat—and this time we'll do it here."

Looked like the gloves were off—if they had ever been on in the first place.

CHAPTER 17

*H*olt stared at the man seated across from him in the interview room. Sebastian Kirkpatrick looked a lot less mournful than he had been when they spoke earlier. He seemed to have gotten over his grief for his wife's death pretty quickly. Now he just seemed angry for having to waste his time at the police station.

"What do you want me to tell you?" he asked in an exasperated tone. "Yes, Ari is my brother-in-law. And no, I don't know where he is right now. Like I told you, I haven't been in touch with him for years. All I know is that he's some kind of gangster, doing some kind of gangster shit. And so I decided a long time ago not to have any dealings with the man. Besides, he never liked me—and the feeling is entirely mutual."

"You didn't think to mention the fact that Margo's brother is a notorious criminal?"

The nightclub owner raised his shoulders. "I didn't think it was relevant. I mean, so the guy is a criminal. So what?"

"Your wife was found in the canal, stabbed to death. I specifically asked you if you had received any threats," said

Holt, leaning forward and tapping the table with his index finger. "The fact that Margo's brother is a criminal strikes me as extremely relevant."

"All right, so maybe I should have mentioned that. But like I said, I didn't think it was important. And besides, I haven't laid eyes on the guy in years. I mean, it's not like we invited him for Christmas dinners or New Year's parties and stuff like that. Last time I saw him was at our wedding, and even back then he scared the bejesus out of me and all of our guests. With the..." He gestured vaguely to the side of his face. "Though God forbid anyone should mention it to him. He was very sensitive about his appearance. Margo once told me he used to beat up kids who made fun of him. He's one scary dude, chief inspector."

Holt leaned back. "So do you think your wife's death may be connected with her brother's dealings? Maybe someone wanted to get back at Ari and targeted his sister instead?"

"I don't think so. Very few people even know that Ari had a sister. And we liked to keep it that way. Besides, she took my name when she married, and for a reason. Though mostly Ari goes by The Atlas these days. Which always struck me as odd, since he hates that nickname. I guess he decided to own it." He gave Holt a dirty look. "Now if that's all, can I go? I've got a business to run, you know. And a wife to bury," he added after a pause, as if his wife's death was nothing but an afterthought.

"Okay, you can go," said Holt. "But if I find out you've been withholding other information from me..."

"I didn't withhold anything. It just slipped my mind," said the man as he got up. "Oh, and you still haven't told me where I need to be to pick up my wife's body."

"We'll let you know," said Holt.

"And why is that, pray tell?"

"Because of the autopsy."

Sebastian seemed taken aback for a moment, but then nodded when the reality of the situation sunk in. "Of course."

After he had left, Holt returned to the office, where Rasheed drew his attention to something else he had discovered.

"Plenty of calls from Margo to one particular number, boss," he said as he pointed to his screen where he had pulled up the victim's phone records. "The guy's name is Orvo Cross. Fitness instructor at the gym where Margo used to go."

"Private lessons, maybe?" Poppy suggested.

"Is that what you kids call it these days?" said Holt.

Poppy stared at him. "You don't think…"

"That's exactly what I think."

Poppy shook her head. "You always think the worst of people. Isn't it possible that he was her personal trainer?"

"It's possible," Holt admitted. "But unlikely, considering the number of phone calls and their length. Let's go and have a chat with Mr. Cross. See if he can't enlighten us to the nature of his relationship with Margo Kirkpatrick."

"Oh, boss," said Rasheed. "There's another number that pops up frequently. A Grace Salomon. Judging from the text messages they exchanged, looks like a personal friend."

"Better go talk to the friend," Holt said. He nodded to his daughter. "And we'll go and see Cross."

As they walked out, he asked Leland, "Any news from the neighborhood canvass?"

"They found the crime scene, boss," said Leland. "Located on Coupure Rechts, close to the house. They also found a witness who claims she heard a scream, followed by a loud splash. This was around eleven last night and corresponds with the location of the crime scene. She looked out of the window, but all she saw was a man dressed in black running away from the scene. She figured it was probably a runner. There's plenty of those around."

"So whoever killed Margo must have snagged her while she was out running and dumped the body in the canal. Did they also find the murder weapon?"

Leland shook his head. "At least now we have a possible time of death, considering Tomas was vague about that."

"We'll probably know more after the post-mortem," said Holt as he grabbed his jacket. "Okay, people, let's move. And remember," he added, "let's be careful out there."

When no one responded, he rolled his eyes. That's what you got when you worked with kids. They didn't know the classics.

CHAPTER 18

*G*eorgina was getting sick and tired of the looks of concern and words of encouragement she was getting from her colleagues. Not that she didn't think it was super sweet that they cared so much about her, but at a certain point, enough was enough. She just wanted to forget that she'd been so stupid not to have noticed that she was being targeted.

She liked to think of herself as a great cop, and her behavior last night was not exactly an advertisement for her talents. And now that the task force had added her to the list of victims, soon the story would be all over the precincts—both local and federal.

In the car, on the drive over, Leland kept casting occasional glances at her. Finally, she'd had enough. "Can you not keep doing that?" she snapped.

"Doing what?" he asked innocently.

"Looking at me as if I'm some kind of victim. I'm fine, Leland. So stop treating me as if I'm made of porcelain, all right?"

"I'm just worried about you, you know," he said as he sank

a little deeper in his seat. She was behind the wheel, having won the coin toss. "You should have seen your face last night. It wasn't pretty."

She had seen her face. Or at least she'd seen the pictures, and Leland was right. She'd looked like death warmed over. Not something she'd ever want her parents to see—or to know about. So she was going to keep this from them. They worried enough about her as it was. No need to feed their imagination.

She softened. "Look, I told you I'm extremely grateful for what you did. If you hadn't been there…" She didn't need to go there. "So let's forget about the whole thing, okay? Let's not mention it ever again. Act like it never happened."

"Do you think that's a good idea? Maybe you *should* talk about it. To process what happened and all of that?"

"I processed it," she said curtly. "Consider it processed."

He didn't look convinced, but she knew he wouldn't bring up the subject unless she broached it. He was a good friend and colleague. "If you say so," he said with a shrug.

They found Margo's friend Grace Salomon at the flower and gift shop that she ran at the Saint Lucas Hospital in town. She was busy with a client, so they patiently waited until she was free. Georgina checked out the magazines and saw that Ruby Floss was on at least three different covers this week. One stated that she had broken up with her boyfriend, one said that she had a heartbreaking secret she wasn't sharing with anyone—except the tabloid's reporter, apparently—and one claimed she was pregnant. For the hundredth time this year.

She rolled her eyes. What was it with people and their obsession with celebrities? But she still picked up the magazine that shouted that Ruby had broken up with her boyfriend and leafed through to the designated pages. Plenty of blurry pictures of Ruby and her boyfriend standing by a pool in some luxury destination, engaged in what could possibly—with a lot of imagination—be construed as a lovers' tiff. In other words: a total nothingburger.

She replaced the magazine when she saw Grace Salomon was free. They approached her, holding out their badges, and asked if they could have a minute of her time to talk about Margo.

The woman's face clouded. "Oh, God. I just heard. Such a terrible thing. How did it happen?"

"I'm afraid we can't share that information," said Georgina. "But know that we're treating her death as suspicious."

"She was murdered? I don't believe this. She was such a sweetheart." She stepped from behind the counter, turned over the Closed sign on the door, and locked it. She crossed her arms in front of her chest and gave them a look of concern. "What do you want to know?"

"You and Margo had been friends a long time?" asked Leland. He had taken out his notebook.

Grace nodded. "We met in high school and had been friends ever since. I was maid of honor at her wedding and she at mine. We even went on vacations together. The whole gang, kids included. She's godmother of my eldest, and I'm godmother of hers. Our lives are so intertwined…" Her voice broke, and a tear rolled down her cheek. "I can't believe she's gone. We were more sisters than friends."

"Do you have any idea who could have done this to her?" asked Georgina. "Someone with a grudge, maybe?"

"No one held a grudge against Margo," said Grace decidedly. "She was the loveliest person in the world. Soft-spoken, kind-hearted. Always ready to lend a helping hand. Her patients adored her. How could they not?"

"Was she in a solid marriage, you think?"

Here Grace showed signs of wavering. "Well…"

"Yes?"

"I'm not sure I should tell you this. Margo probably wouldn't like for anyone to know—especially the kids."

"It's important," said Georgina. "Anything that can shed some light on why this happened to her."

"You want us to catch whoever is responsible, don't you?" said Leland. And that decided her.

"She and Sebastian had been leading separate lives for years. Him with his girlfriends," she scoffed. "She once confronted him about it, and he said it was all part of being a nightclub owner. Projecting an image. It didn't mean anything. But obviously, it did to her."

"So Sebastian had affairs?"

"Yeah, and plenty of them. The first one—at least that Margo knew about—was that singer." She gestured to the magazine stand. "Ruby Floss."

"Are they still an item?"

She shook her head. "This was a long time ago. They both moved on. She with her many boyfriends," she said, gesturing to the magazine stand. "And Sebastian with skanks he met at his clubs. You know the type," she added scornfully. "Not the type of women you want to introduce to your kids. Which is why he usually pretended to be husband of the year."

"And what about Margo? Was she also having an affair?" asked Georgina, remembering the many calls to the woman's fitness instructor.

Once again, Grace hesitated, then finally nodded. "There's this guy named Orvo Cross. She met him at the fitness club. He was her personal trainer, and then he became her personal something else. I told her to watch out for him, as he always struck me as a real player. Probably has affairs with all of his clients, you know. He once tried it on with me, but I said no, and showed him my wedding ring. But I guess

Margo was feeling lonely and neglected. So she was an easy target. She was crazy about him—totally in love."

"What about Margo's brother?" asked Leland. "What can you tell us about him?"

Grace lifted a perfectly plucked eyebrow. She was a handsome woman with blond hair and a full figure. "You mean the gangster? They weren't in touch. No way was she going to let that kind of darkness and violence into her life. Back when we were in high school, I could tell there was something wrong with Ari. He was the kind of kid that would extort money from other kids, you know, and pick fights with people. He was expelled from school, of course, which was a good thing for Margo, as his behavior couldn't reflect badly on her anymore. And then things went from bad to worse."

"Do you think that Margo's death might be connected to her brother's criminal activities?" asked Leland.

Grace shook her head. "I doubt it. Like I said, they hadn't been in touch for years. Margo didn't want anything to do with that man, for the sake of her family and their safety."

"Do you think he might target his own sister?"

"Oh, absolutely not. Ari may be a tough gangster these days, but he would never hurt his own family. Never, never, never."

"Okay, thanks, Grace," said Georgina. She handed the woman her card. "If there's anything you can think of that might be relevant, please give me a call, all right?"

Grace stared at the card. "It's the kids I worry about, you know. They adored their mom. This is gonna hit them hard."

CHAPTER 19

⹅

$\mathcal{W}$hen they arrived at Boutique Fitness, Poppy had to admit that she liked what she saw. She'd been going to the gym in Loveringem, but now that she lived in Ghent, it had been a while since she'd been.

"Looking for a new fitness club, huh?" said her dad as he found her admiring the gym's exterior.

"We could come together," she suggested. She had been trying to persuade her dad to join a gym for the longest time. He needed the exercise and also the distraction. Right now, her dad lived for his job—apart from the one hobby he had in collecting comics—and that wasn't healthy in her book.

"I get plenty of exercise walking Harley," he said.

"Dad, you need at least half an hour of elevated-heart-rate activity a day."

"My heart rate rises every time I walk into the precinct," he said. "So I'm good, thanks."

"I'm getting their price list," she said as they walked in. The club she was going to now was cheap and also great for her purpose. She didn't need fancy lessons or a personalized approach. As long as she could spend an hour on one of the fitness machines, she was fine. Unfortunately, it wasn't part of a chain, so it didn't have a club in Ghent.

As they approached the desk, she searched around for a price list and, to her surprise, couldn't find one. When a slim girl with a ponytail joined them, she asked, "Do you have a price list, please?"

The girl's toothy smile didn't change. "We don't work like that," she said.

She frowned. "What do you mean you don't work like that? You have prices, don't you?"

"We do, but they're all personally tailored."

Her frown deepened. "I don't understand," she admitted.

The girl must have had this conversation countless times, for she didn't even bat an eye. "What I would suggest is you have a conversation with one of our personal trainers, and he'll explain everything to you. I'll book you an appointment right now if you like."

"I don't need a personal trainer," she said. "I just want to use the machines."

"Nevertheless, if you want to become a member, you need to have an intake interview first, so we can see what your needs are and tailor the program accordingly."

"Look, all I want is to—"

But before she could finish the sentence, her dad had flipped out his badge and slapped it down on the counter. He never did have a lot of patience.

"Police," he grunted. "Chief Inspector Holt and Inspector Holt. We need to speak with one of your trainers. Orvo Cross. Is he on the premises?"

For the first time, the girl's smile wavered. "He is, but he's busy with a client right now. So if you could take a seat over there—"

"We're not taking a seat," said Holt as he walked right on through. There was a barrier, and as he cut a steely look at the girl, she quickly pressed a button, and the barrier lifted to grant them access. "Where can we find Mr. Cross?"

"Um, he's in training area number one. The red zone."

"Thanks," he grunted and entered the hallowed halls of the fitness club, Poppy right on his heels.

"I don't get it," she lamented. "How can they not have a price list?"

"Didn't you hear the lady? They don't work like that."

"That's just a load of nonsense. All I need is access to an elliptical and a couple of those fancy weightlifting machines. I don't need an intake interview or whatever it's called."

He cocked his eyebrow in her direction. "We're here to conduct an interview with Orvo Cross, honey. Not negotiate a gym membership."

"Maybe we can ask him, though. At the end of the interview? Or maybe at the beginning. To break the ice?"

"Let's not," he suggested, then frowned as they suddenly found themselves in a pretty large area teeming with fitness fanatics going about their business of getting into shape.

"Oh, wow," she said, immediately excited. "I think I'm going to like it here." Her old club had been small, with only a couple of people present any time she managed to get in there. This place was rocking! "You *have* to join up, Dad. Can't you feel the buzz?"

"I can feel the bullshit," Holt grumbled. "Now where the hell is this red zone?"

"Ooh, they even have a spa," she said as she spotted a sign that said Pool & Sauna Area.

Instead of checking the entire place, Holt tapped a beefcake on the shoulder. The guy snapped his head up as if stung, but when he clocked the stocky chief inspector, quickly simmered down again. "Wassup, buddy?" he asked.

"Where can I find the red zone?" asked Holt.

The guy pointed in the general direction of the back of the large gym space. "They're the private booths at the back," he said. "Just follow the red line on the floor."

They both stared down at the rubber-matted floor, and now Poppy saw it: there were several lines drawn there in different colors, like at the hospital.

"Easy as pie," Holt muttered as he thanked the guy and started following the red line.

"I bet this place is expensive," said Poppy as she hurried after her dad, who was setting a fast pace. "With all the amenities, I'm betting it's a lot more expensive than my old club."

"You don't need this fancy-schmancy club, honey," her dad agreed. "All you need is a basic club that won't set you back a month's salary for the privilege of prancing around in a leotard and pretending you're hot shit."

"Leotards are for ballet, Dad. At the club, you wear gym shorts and a T-shirt."

"Whatever. It still makes you look like a pansy."

"Dad! Language!"

They had finally arrived at this famous red zone, and without preamble, Holt placed his hand on the handle of the glass door and burst into the room. The two people present looked up in surprise. One was a middle-aged woman, and the other was a gorgeous male specimen who could only be Orvo Cross.

"Holt," said Holt curtly, holding up his badge. "Police. We need to talk to you, Cross."

The fitness trainer blinked at them. "Can't this wait? I'm in the middle of a session."

Holt held his gaze for all of five seconds before the guy buckled under the intensity. "Okay, all right. Kimmy, darling," he said, addressing the client, "we'll have to postpone the rest of our session, all right? But not to worry. You did great. So why don't you spend half an hour on the elliptical, and I'll see you tomorrow."

The woman didn't seem particularly annoyed with the interruption, and if the high color of her cheeks and the dark V-line of sweat on her T-shirt were any indication, she probably had had her fill of Orvo's ministrations for the day. She hurried out, giving both Holt and Poppy curious glances as she did.

"What's this about?" asked the trainer, who was one of those dark, handsome men, in addition to being ridiculously muscular. Poppy wouldn't mind having a session with him, even if it did cost her an arm and a leg.

"We're investigating the death of Margo Kirkpatrick," said Holt. "She was one of your clients?"

"She was, yeah," said Orvo. He didn't even seem remotely surprised by the news that Margo was dead. Probably he'd already been told. The story had been in the online version of several papers and also on AVS, their local TV station.

"We've also spoken to Margo's friend Grace," said Holt. "And according to her, you and Margo were having an affair?"

The guy, who had been wiping the sweat off his neck with a towel, paused in mid-wipe. "She said that?"

"She did," Holt confirmed. "So can you tell us about your relationship with Mrs. Kirkpatrick, Mr. Cross?"

"There isn't much to tell," he said, adopting a more sheepish attitude now. "We had an affair, it's true. Though I hope you will treat this information as confidential."

"You wouldn't want word to get out that you were sleeping with one of your clients?"

The man had the good decency to flinch. "It's not a habit," he assured them.

"You mean you don't sleep with all of your clients? I'm glad to hear it."

"Look, Margo was lonely. Her marriage was on the rocks, and she longed for some affection. Plus, she was a good-looking woman, and we had a connection."

"She was also a very wealthy woman." Between her orthodontic dentistry practice and her husband's nightclubs, the Kirkpatricks were certainly very well off.

The trainer's eyes flashed with annoyance. "I didn't care about her money. That's not what this was about."

"You're not going to tell me this was love?"

"Well, it was certainly not about the money. I cared for her, and she cared for me. That's all this was. No, it wasn't a great love affair. Just an innocent fling, you know."

"Your messages were very... passionate," said Holt.

That was an understatement. Rasheed had sent them a list of messages that the dentist exchanged with her personal trainer, and stuff really got pretty heated—and graphic.

"Are you in the habit of sending all of your clients images of yourself in a state of full arousal, Mr. Cross?"

"Of course not," said the man. "Like I said, we liked each other. We had fun together. But it didn't go beyond that."

"So just a fun fling," said Holt. "Can you think of any reason why someone would hurt Margo?"

"None whatsoever. She was a lovely person, and as far as I know, she didn't have any enemies." He frowned. "Why? You think this was a deliberate attack? I thought it was a mugging or something? Someone attacked her while she was out jogging?"

"We're still looking at all the different scenarios," said Holt. "She never mentioned her brother, for instance?"

The man's bewilderment was genuine. "Her brother? No, she didn't mention him."

"How about her husband? Did she talk about the state of her marriage?"

"Not really. We didn't talk much, you know." A grin slid up his features. "We spent most of our time together enjoying each other's company—if you know what I mean."

"Where did you do this enjoying?" asked Poppy.

"At my place," said the guy. "I live around the corner. She figured it wasn't a good idea to meet at hers. Her husband works strange hours. He owns a couple of nightclubs."

"Do you know if her husband was aware of your affair?" asked Holt.

"I don't think so. We were always careful. Even though she said her husband probably wouldn't care if he did find out. She said he was playing around behind her back and didn't try to hide it. The reason she was being careful was more about protecting her kids. She didn't want them to know neither of their parents gave a hoot about their marriage."

"Okay, thanks, Mr. Cross," said Holt as he made to leave.

But Poppy wasn't going to miss her chance just because her dad was done with the trainer. "Can I ask you one more thing, Mr. Cross?"

"Sure," said the guy, noticeably more friendly to her than to her dad. "Shoot."

"I was thinking of becoming a member here. Can you tell me how much that would cost?"

Holt rolled his eyes, but she stood her ground.

The trainer smiled. "It doesn't work like that, inspector."

"Look, all I want to know is how much I need to pay to use the elliptical and some of the weightlifting machines."

"I'd say that would probably set you back about a hundred bucks. But then you wouldn't have the benefit of a personal trainer who will gauge your fitness levels and create a program that is tailor-made just for you and your fitness level."

"I don't need all of that," she assured him, though now that she knew what this guy's extracurricular activities entailed, maybe it was worth it to pay the extra money? But then she immediately nixed the thought. She was happy with Bernard. She didn't need a fling with Mr. Hottie Cross—no way.

"Okay, then I guess a hundred is the price," he said.

"That's a lot of money," she said. "My last club only cost twenty-five. What would I get for four times that?"

"Oh, where do I begin?" said the guy, his smile widening. He was on familiar terrain now. "For one thing, all Boutique Fitness subscriptions include access to the pool and sauna area, and on top of that—"

"Okay, thanks for your time, Mr. Cross," said Holt, who clearly had heard all he needed to hear. "And if you can think of anything that might be important, please give me a call."

"A hundred bucks!" she said as they legged it back to the entrance. "I don't care if he throws in personal massages. That's a lot of money for a gym membership."

"All the more reason to pick a different club. Or no club at all. Did you know that climbing stairs is considered one of the best aerobic exercises? And guess what building has lots and lots of stairs? Federal Police headquarters! All the fitness training you need—and it won't cost you a cent."

"You're so funny, dad. Did anyone ever tell you about your great sense of humor?"

"Never," he admitted.

"That's because you don't have one!"

Holt's phone buzzed again, and he took it out of his pocket. "God, not again," he moaned as he showed Poppy the display.

"Just pick up, Dad," she suggested. "She clearly wants to tell you about the baby, so you better let her."

With as much excitement as he could muster, he pressed the green button. "Leah," he said morosely. Then he frowned. "Slow down. Who threw what through your window?" He locked eyes with his daughter. "We'll be there in twenty minutes."

"What's going on?" asked Poppy.

Holt was already legging it in the direction of the car. "Some nut threw a brick through your mom's window!"

CHAPTER 20

The Holts arrived at the same time as Terrence did. As Holt's ex-boss got out of his car, Holt got out of his. The two men barely acknowledged each other as they both hurried up to the front door of the house where Holt used to live with his wife.

Leah appeared before they reached the door, looking extremely distraught. "I don't need this crap, you know," she said as she greeted both her new husband and her ex. "Not in the state I'm in. Doctor Osgood told me to take it easy. No stress, he said." She gestured to the window. "I call this stressful, wouldn't you? Very stressful!"

Holt examined the window. Someone had indeed thrown a brick right through it, and a sizable brick too, judging from the damage.

"Christ," said Terrence as he dragged a hand through his graying and thinning mane. He looked a lot older than he had the last time Holt had seen him. That's what being married to Leah did to a man, he thought, but then chided himself for being so negative about his ex-wife. Like Poppy had told him time and time again, he should simply forgive and forget.

He was trying. Lord knew he was trying. But she wasn't exactly helping.

He and Terrence walked into the house and into the living room, off the hallway to the right.

They stared at the brick, which lay on the Persian rug, surrounded by splintered glass.

"There's something written on there," Terrence remarked.

"What is it?" asked Holt as he tried to make out the writing.

"Police… killed…" said Terrence. "Shall I turn it over?"

"Yeah, but carefully," said Holt. "Don't touch it."

Terrence used a shard of glass to turn the brick over.

"Margo," Terrence said.

"Police killed Margo," said Holt. "But…" He looked up at his old boss. "Margo Kirkpatrick was killed last night. You don't think…"

Terrence pointed to a strange mark on the brick. "That's the mark of The Atlas," he said.

For a moment, neither man spoke. Then Holt said, "The Atlas is accusing the police of murdering his sister?" When Terrence gave him a guilty look, he added, "You did this?"

"No, of course not!" Terrence said. "Do you really think I'd go around murdering perfectly innocent dentists?"

Poppy had joined them, and also Leah. When Poppy saw the mess the brick had made, she cried, "They killed Missy!"

Missy was the toy dog that Leah knitted back when Poppy was a baby. She'd been very attached to that dog and had slept with it for years, well into her teen years. And so Leah had put it on the windowsill, next to an arrangement of pictures. There were no pictures of Holt, though, as far as he could see. Even the ones that had featured him and Leah and

Poppy now only showed Poppy and Leah, with him cut neatly out of the frame.

"He'll live," commented Holt. Who wouldn't live if he didn't start telling him the truth was Terrence. He grabbed the man's lapels. "Better start talking, Terrence."

"Oh, bugger off, Holt," Terrence grunted as he yanked himself loose and got up. "I didn't do this and you know it."

"So why does The Atlas think you did?"

"Because he's a psychopathic maniac?"

"What's this all about?" asked Leah.

"Yeah, can someone please explain to me what's going on?" asked Poppy as she fished Missy from the rubble and picked some shards of glass from the tattered doll doggy.

"The Atlas thinks that the police killed his sister," said Holt. "And that's why he threw this brick through your window."

"And I just told Holt that he's mistaken," said Terrence.

"Wait, who's The Atlas? And who is his sister?" asked Leah.

"The Atlas is a criminal," said Poppy. "Whose sister was found murdered this morning. And for some reason, he thinks that the police were behind her murder." She frowned at her stepdad. "And why does he think that, Terrence?"

Terrence rubbed his cheek. He looked harried. "Look, there's this rumor going around that we killed Margo Kirkpatrick to draw out her brother, all right? Hoping he'd attend her funeral, and that way we can nail him. But it's just a stupid rumor!"

"Swear to me that's all this is, Terrence," said Holt, once again attaching himself to his old boss's collar.

"Will you let go of me, you brute!"

"Can you boys stop fighting please?" said Leah in that typical high voice she got that betrayed her annoyance. "This isn't what I need right now!" she added as she placed her hands on her belly. "In my state!"

"Okay, fine," said Holt. "So you didn't kill The Atlas's sister. But then who did?"

"How should I know?" Terrence cried. "You're the detective, Holt. You figure it out. And while you're at it, try to get it through that thick skull of her brother's that it wasn't us!"

"Stop yelling!!!" Leah yelled, her face blotchy.

"Yes, Missy doesn't like it when you yell," said Poppy as she stroked her old doll's head affectionately.

"Now you're both going to clean this up," said Leah. And when Holt and Terrence made protesting sounds, she raised her voice again. "Right this minute!"

"Fine," Holt murmured.

"Great," Terrence added.

And so he and his old boss were forced to work together to clean up the mess that The Atlas had made. But first they had to wait for the crime scene people that had been called in to try and extract any evidence they could find, something that didn't sit well with Leah at all. And while they sat on the couch sipping from cups of coffee that Poppy had made, Terrence heaved a deep sigh. "This isn't easy for me, you know, Holt."

"Of course it is," said Holt. "You're living in my old house, sleeping with my wife, and now you're having a kid with her. Of course it's easy."

The guy rubbed the side of his face. "I never expected to become a dad again. Pretty soon I'll be knee-deep in diapers and getting up at all hours to settle down a screaming baby."

Holt grinned. "Serves you right. Karma in action."

"Make fun as much as you want, but this affects you too."

"How do you figure that? I'm out of the picture, Terrence."

"Oh, no, you're not. Leah still sees you as part of the

family. So when this baby is born, you'll have to pitch in, same as me."

"Out of the question. This has nothing to do with me."

"You wish."

Holt knew that Terrence was probably right. The fact that Leah kept calling him was evidence that she wasn't done with him. Not by a mile. She had always been extremely family-oriented, and apparently she still saw him in that light, in spite of the divorce.

"So…" Terrence cleared his throat as he leaned in. "So how is she? As a mother, I mean?"

Holt slowly turned to take him in. "Are you serious?"

Terrence held his gaze. "You went through this with her—twice. So tell me: what is it like?"

Holt sighed deeply. "There's one thing you need to understand about Leah, and that is that she's a mother first and foremost. The wife part is a distant second. Her children mean everything to her. The man who made them? Not so much. So expect your entire lives to revolve around this baby from now on." He wagged a finger at the man. "And you better be prepared to see this through, Terrence—or else…"

"Oh, I'll see this through," said Terrence quietly. "I mean, did I expect to become a dad at age fifty-six? Definitely not. But now that I am, and I've had time to get used to the idea…" His crusty features broke into a smile. "It's gonna be great, Holt." He patted Holt's arm. "With you being the kid's godfather."

His head whipped around so fast he felt a definite crick. "What!"

"That's what Leah's been trying to tell you. And if you didn't keep hanging up on her, she would have by now."

"But I don't *want* to be your baby's godfather!"

"Hey, this is your ex-wife we're talking about," said

Terrence. "This is what Leah wants, so this is what Leah gets. She has this idea it will reunite the family. Heal the rift."

"God help us all," he muttered.

"Well, that's the whole idea."

Holt's son had entered the living room and for a moment just stared at his dad and stepdad seated side by side on the couch. It was indeed a strange and rare sight.

"Hey, buddy," said Terrence.

"Hey, son," said Holt.

"Dad," said Aaron. "And... Dad."

"This is what it's all about, Holt," said Terrence as he got up. "Now talk to your boy. Heal that rift. I for one have forgiven you... more or less," he added as he rubbed his jaw where Holt's right hook had done considerable damage that time.

Aaron took in the devastation The Atlas had wrought, and then let himself drop down next to his dad. "At least they didn't throw in a petrol bomb or a grenade or something."

"Yeah, at least there's that," Holt agreed. He was pleasantly surprised that his son was talking to him again. The first couple of months after the divorce Aaron had pretended he didn't have a dad, so this was all to the good.

"So what's all this about a baby?" asked his son.

"It sure is news to me."

"Are you all right with it, though?" asked Aaron as he studied him for a moment.

"I guess. I mean, it's not really my business anymore, you know. It's your mom and Terrence's now. How about you? How do you feel about getting another sister?"

Aaron shrugged. "Same as you. It's got nothing to do with me. It's mom's business and Terrence's. But if it makes them happy, I guess it's all right with me."

"Your mother will need all the help she can get," said Holt. He remembered how Leah got when she was pregnant with

Poppy and Aaron both. A little manic and a whole lot of crazy. He hadn't wanted to tell Terrence, not to send him running to the hills, but Leah was high-maintenance, and never more so than when she was pregnant.

"That goes for you, too, Dad," said Aaron as he clapped him on the back. "Or haven't you noticed how she's trying to reel you back in after she first kicked you out? She's one clever operator, that woman. It takes a village, and we're the village."

He couldn't help but grimace at the thought that soon he'd be a new dad by proxy. It must have tickled his son's funny bone, for Aaron laughed loudly at the expression on his dad's face.

It was like music to his ears.

CHAPTER 21

*W*hen Holt and Poppy got back to the precinct, Roy was waiting for them. He was actually seated behind Holt's desk, which was normally a big no-no. But not for Roy, who was probably Holt's oldest friend and colleague. Just to be on the safe side, he got up the moment they walked in, though.

"Trouble in paradise?" he asked as Holt approached.

"Yeah, The Atlas just threw a brick through Leah's window, accusing Terrence of murdering his sister. Terrence assured me it isn't true." He fixed his friend with a look. "What do you think?"

Roy shrugged. "I mean, is Terrence capable of doing a thing like that? I'd say yeah, of course he is. But if he did, no one at the station is aware of it. And he's not the kind of guy who'd go around murdering people with his own hands. Stabbed with a knife, was she?"

"Yeah, stabbed several times in the throat."

"That's not Terrence. If he were to personally kill a person he'd use a gun. Nice and clean. And make sure he doesn't get any blood spatter on his person. Knives definitely aren't his thing."

"Yeah, that's what I figured," said Holt as he made to drop down into his chair. But before he could, Roy hooked his arm through his and led him in the direction of the door. "Where are we going?"

"I need a smoke," Roy confessed. "And a chat," he added once they were out of earshot of the rest of the team.

Holt wondered if Roy was going to confess that it *was* the police who were behind the murder of The Atlas's sister. Instead, it was something else entirely.

Once they had reached the smoking area, which was the inner courtyard of the building, he said, "It's Poppy."

Holt's heart leaped. Anything to do with his daughter had the power to make him lose his cool. He still managed to sound reasonably chill when he responded, "What about her?"

"Okay, so you have to be honest with me here, Holt," said Roy as he took a pack of cigarettes from his pocket and tapped one out. He offered Holt one, but he declined. He'd managed to shake the habit years ago, when the kids were born and Leah had demanded he quit smoking or else, and he wasn't going to get started again. "This new boyfriend of hers. What do you think? Thumbs up or thumbs down? I need to know."

Holt grinned with relief. "What are you, a Roman emperor?"

"You know what I mean. I'm the girl's godfather, for Christ's sakes. If I didn't have her best interests at heart, that would make me a pretty lousy one, wouldn't you say?"

Holt thought for a moment, and decided to be honest. "At first I didn't like him. But now I'm thinking maybe he's all right, you know. I mean, this is Poppy we're talking about.

She probably knows best. And so I'm willing to take a chance on the guy. For her sake."

"That's very generous of you, Holt," said Roy. "Considering the last guy broke her heart—remember?"

"I probably should have broken his legs," Holt grunted as his eyes narrowed at the recollection. But then Poppy wouldn't have wanted that. After all, if he was going around breaking the legs of every kid who ever broke his daughter's heart, he'd probably have a full-time job. Plus, he'd be out of a job. Maybe once upon a time cops could get away with things like that, but not these days.

"Okay, so I'm guessing you already ran a background check on the kid?"

"I didn't, and I advise you not to either. It's illegal."

"As if you'd care," Roy scoffed, but when Holt gave him a look, he held up his hands. "Okay, fine. I won't."

"If Poppy found out, she'd never forgive me," he said. Once upon a time he'd have done a background check on every single one of her boyfriends, but Poppy had drummed it into him that he should have a little faith in his daughter's choices.

And she was right, of course. She was a clever girl.

"Okay, then I guess that's it," said Roy as he took a long drag from his cancer stick. "I don't have to keep tabs on the kid."

"You were planning to put him under surveillance?"

"Something like that. Not officially, of course. But I could have put a couple of my men to follow him around for a couple of days. Just to make sure he's on the up and up. But if you're telling me not to, then I won't."

"Nah, Poppy wouldn't appreciate it," said Holt.

"She wouldn't know." But when Holt gave him another one of his famous looks, he grinned. "Of course she'd know.

She'd probably recognize my guys, no matter how careful and circumspect they tried to be."

"That's my daughter," he said, and didn't hide his sense of pride. He loved both his kids equally, but if he was totally honest, Poppy inspired his sense of parental pride just that little bit more. Though possibly that was because she had chosen the same career path, and he worked with her every day now.

"So are you trying to catch The Atlas?" asked Roy.

"Why, you are also after him?"

"Absolutely. There's an entire cell dedicated to taking down him and his organization. Which is why we know that you and Poppy were staking out that clinic last night."

"Great minds think alike," said Holt.

"I think he's ready to get rid of that port-wine stain," said Roy. "It's been bothering him long enough. Plus, rumor has it that he's ready to disappear. Leave his operation to his second-in-command and move to Dubai or some other place to live out his retirement and enjoy his hard-earned fortune."

"But he can't do that looking the way he does," Holt said, nodding. "So it's probably him that kidnapped that doctor."

"Like you said: great minds think alike."

"Boss?" said Rasheed the moment Holt stepped back into the office. He walked over to the detective's desk. "I managed to retrieve the deleted messages from Margo Kirkpatrick's phone." He pointed to the screen. "What was it that fitness guy called their relationship? A harmless fling?"

Holt's eyes flicked across the screen. His mood darkened, like it always did when people lied to him. "Poppy," he barked. "Have a couple of uniforms pick up Mr. Orvo Cross. Looks like he hasn't been entirely honest with us!"

CHAPTER 22

For the second time that day, Poppy was enjoying the pleasure of studying Orvo Cross's uniquely attractive features. Though this time the fitness trainer wasn't in his natural habitat but found himself in one of the small and significantly less pleasant interview rooms the precinct was the proud owner of. A dark green fungus was slowly taking over the ceiling, and the walls had fur growing on them. The man himself didn't look so great either. Even his hair, which had been nicely gelled and defying the laws of gravity, had drooped.

"Okay, so maybe I didn't mention that little thing," he admitted. "But I don't see the significance. As far as I'm concerned, it *was* a fling."

"So the fact that Margo said she was going to divorce her husband and marry you didn't strike you as significant?" asked Holt as he slapped a printed-out copy of Margo's deleted messages in front of the woman's lover.

"She wanted to take things to the next level, but I didn't," said the fitness trainer, placing a hand on his chest. "I wasn't in love with her, and that's what I told her. But she said she was going to go ahead with the divorce plans anyway, whether I liked it or not. I mean, talk about delusional."

"So leading your clients on is all fine and dandy, until they fall in love with you and want to make things serious," said Poppy, who was starting to dislike this man to such an extent she didn't think she'd feel comfortable becoming a client at his gym. He'd been stringing Margo along, and when she fell for him, sent her packing. "Did you break up with her?"

"No, I didn't," said the guy. "I didn't see the need. Like I told her, I liked the way things were going between us. I didn't want to marry her, but I also didn't want to break up with her. And so what if she was going to divorce her husband? I wasn't going to marry her—ever."

"Why did she delete these messages, you think?" asked Holt.

"Probably to hide them from her husband? What went on between him and Margo wasn't any of my business. I got the impression things hadn't been going well for a long time, and the only reason they stayed together was for the kids. But now that they were all grown up and moved out of the house, nothing was stopping her from divorcing the guy."

"Can you tell us where you were last night around eleven, Mr. Cross?" asked Holt.

The man's eyes went wide. "You don't think I killed her, do you? I mean, I could have simply broken up with her if I wanted to. I didn't have to kill her to get rid of her."

"Just answer the question," said Poppy sternly.

"I was at the club, working late," he said.

"You were with a client at that late hour?"

"I was, yeah. The club is open until ten-thirty, but sometimes I take on clients after hours for a private session. You can ask her, if you like. She'll vouch for me."

"This private session, was it in the same vein as the sessions you gave Margo?" asked Holt.

The guy had the audacity to offer them a smirk. "Can I help it that I'm Mr. Popular? I mean," he added as he gestured to himself. "Who doesn't want a piece of this, right?" When they both stared at him, stunned at the audacity, he quickly piped down. "I'm just kidding. It was just a regular session. Of course it was. I'm not going to do... that... at the club."

"Just get lost," said Holt as he got up. "Now!"

Once the trainer had left, Poppy conferred with her dad. "What do you think?" he asked.

"I think he's probably too stupid to be Margo's killer," she determined. "I mean, as much as it pains me to say this, I just don't think he has it in him. Like he said, he could have simply broken up with her if he wanted to. He didn't need to kill her."

"Yeah, I agree," said Holt. "And it's not as if he has a family or anything. So Margo suddenly pressuring him to get married wouldn't have affected him as much as it would a married man." He balled his hands into fists. "I would love to nail that guy, though. God, how I would love to make the arrest and wipe that smug smile off his face."

"One thing's for sure," said Poppy.

"What's that?"

"I'll never join his gym. Are you kidding me?" she added when her dad laughed. "With that guy hanging around? Maybe all of their trainers are like that. The sexy-stalky type."

"Yeah, Mr. Cross isn't exactly an advertisement for the Boutique Gym. But then again, it isn't illegal to seduce women and have affairs with them. So unless his alibi doesn't check out, I guess we can cross him off our list of suspects."

They walked out into the open office where the team was housed, and Poppy got busy updating the big crime board with all the latest information. A small section of the board was dedicated to the abduction of Dr. McMinn, though apart from the fact that The Atlas was a suspect in the kidnapping and his sister had been murdered that morning, there wasn't really much of a connection.

There might be, though, Poppy thought. And if there was, they'd find it, she was sure of it. Even though her dad often said she was way too optimistic for his taste, she felt that being optimistic was a boon for police investigations and she'd die on that hill every day. In a manner of speaking, obviously.

CHAPTER 23

*B*arney Waller had been going about his business as he always did: a bit of shopping, then arriving home to cook a frugal meal over the stove. He'd heard good things about the Moulinex Cookeo, a kind of crockpot, but the price was way too steep for his modest budget. Will Canavan, a friend of his, had assured him that he'd be able to get him one for a good price from the local thrift store, but so far none had popped up yet.

Probably the people who owned these Cookeos held on to them, which proved how great they were.

He looked up when he heard a strange noise. Almost as if someone was walking on the deck. As he glanced through the window, he didn't see anything though, so probably he was simply hearing things that weren't there, as sometimes happened.

Once he'd finished his meal, which consisted of a random collection of veggies thrown in a pot and stewed with some ground beef, tomato sauce and plenty of seasoning, he settled in front of the television, his trusty stray calico on his lap. He preferred the shows with plenty of singing and dancing rather than movies or TV shows. His favorite show was *The Masked Singer*, since you got singing *and* dancing for the price of one. Once the show was over, he decided to turn in for the night. And he was brushing his teeth when he heard that same sound of the floorboards on deck creaking as if someone was moving around up there.

Only this time when he glanced out of the window, a man stared right back at him. It was the same man he'd seen in the canal barge moored next to him.

Like the night before, he didn't look happy to see him. At all!

And as he tried to figure out what to do, suddenly there was a heavy knock at the door, then another one, and then the door swung off its hinges and the man stood there.

"You... you can't just come in here," he said weakly as he glanced around for some kind of weapon to defend himself. "This is... this is private property, you know."

When he was still sleeping rough he always kept a knife close by for these types of situations. Even though he didn't think he could kill a man, a stab to the leg might slow an attacker down long enough for him to make his escape. But where was that knife now? Oh, curse the easy life! He'd gotten soft in his old age, and now look where it had gotten him!

As the man towered over him, he knew that he was in a whole big lot of trouble!

* * *

HOLT AND POPPY were back staking out the McMinn clinic. Like the night before, Poppy had bought a sizable portion of French fries, only this time she'd ignored her dad's protestations and bought him one as well, so he wouldn't eat hers.

Not that she begrudged him a few, but the man had such an appetite he was capable of eating half her portion.

"These are even better than the ones you got yesterday," he said.

"They're the exact same ones, Dad. Exactly the same."

"They can't be the same. Different taters. Different oil. Different person making them."

"Same taters, same oil, same person."

"All the same, these are much better."

She merely shook her head. There was simply no arguing with this man. He always had to be right, even when he was wrong. But that's what you got when you worked with your dad and he was also your superior officer.

"Bernard had to work late again?"

"Yep. Bernard always has to work late, Dad. That's because he's a bartender at a nightclub. Nightclubs open at night, as the name implies." They'd had this conversation.

"Maybe he could get a different job? That way you two can be together some of the time. As opposed to now, where you never see each other."

"We see each other plenty. And besides, there's something to be said about not seeing too much of each other."

"Is there? Your mom always used to complain she never saw enough of me."

"Bernard doesn't have to find a different job," she said. "Not on my account. If he wants to change jobs, that's great. But if not, that's also great. It's called giving each other the space you need to be the person you want to be. And not trying to run the other person's life."

"Huh. Must be something new," he quipped.

"So about Mom being pregnant, huh?" she said, trying to steer the conversation away from herself and her boyfriend.

"Yeah," he said curtly. "Turns out that she wants me to be

the kid's godfather. And Terrence agrees with her." He groaned. "Soon I'll be changing diapers again."

"That'll be a first," she said with a grin.

"I'll have you know that I changed plenty of diapers back in the day. Plenty. And I'm sure I still have the hang of it."

"Mom will have us all changing diapers."

"She's a real taskmaster, that one."

They glanced out of the window at the clinic, but all was quiet. No one coming or going, and no lights on inside. Whatever The Atlas was up to, he wasn't doing it tonight.

Poppy turned on the radio just in time for the DJ to announce that Ruby Floss had decided to postpone her European tour for personal reasons. Ruby's latest song sounded through the car, causing Holt to wince. "Can't you put on something good?" he complained.

"This is good," she argued. "The best."

"I beg to differ." But since all of those fries had clearly had a mellowing effect on his mood, he made no other attempts to get her to change the channel, and so they sat together companionably as they finished their midnight meals and listened to some great tunes.

Being on a stake-out wasn't as bad as people made it out to be.

CHAPTER 24

Somehow—he didn't exactly know how—Georgina had convinced Leland to return to the Marquee. Even though he had explained why this was a really bad idea, somehow he now found himself seated to the side of the same bar where only twenty-four hours ago his partner had been drugged. Only this time, he wasn't going to allow his vigilance to waver for even a single fraction of a millisecond. Like a hawk, he kept a close eye on her.

To be fair to Georgina, she had promised she wasn't going to try and bait her attacker into spiking her drink a second night in a row. Instead, she was simply going to keep an eye out for the guy, in the hope of recognizing him, and so was Leland. And since the attacker most likely had clocked Leland even as Leland had clocked him, Georgina had convinced him to wear a disguise in the form of a wispy mustache and a pair of thick-framed glasses.

He hated the 'stache—oh, how he hated it. He had checked himself in the mirror before setting out on this stake-out, and it made him look stupid and ugly. He wasn't a handsome man to begin with, and the mustache made him look even worse. Even Rasheed had looked startled when he had suddenly found himself in close proximity to the mustache.

"Wha-wha-what is that thing?" Rasheed asked, staring at the hirsute appendage with a touch of concern, as if afraid it was going to dislodge itself from its parent body and go on a rampage.

"It's a disguise," he said morosely. "Georgina thinks it's a good idea, so..."

"And you always do what Georgina tells you to do?"

It was a good question. And it was one he didn't have an answer to. Carefully analyzing the evidence, it would appear that he did always do what Georgina told him to. Though he knew how bad that sounded, and how weak it made him look. So he said, "Of course not. I'm my own man. It just felt like a good idea to wear a disguise this time, that's all. My decision," he added for good measure, though he knew it sounded lame.

Rasheed gave him a look of commiseration. "Do you want me to come?"

"No, it's fine," he said. "I'm sure we can manage."

"I'll come," said Rasheed. "We don't want the same thing to happen again, now do we?"

"No, we most certainly don't want that," he agreed.

And so he now sat to one side of the bar, well hidden from view, wearing the hideous mustache and the equally hideous pair of glasses, while Rasheed leaned against the wall and made sure he kept a low profile as well. Between the two of them, they had a perfect overview of the bar, and if the rapist returned, they'd clock him, no question.

Georgina, meanwhile, had taken up the same position at the bar and was carefully scanning her surroundings for a sign of the man who had drugged her the night before. Leland had to hand it to her: the woman possessed a mighty set of brass balls. Probably a bigger set than any man he knew, and that included himself.

Suddenly Georgina gave him the agreed-upon sign, and he narrowed his eyes to try and see what was going on. Just at that moment, there was some kind of commotion at the bar, with several people trying to order drinks at the same time, and the throng obscured his view. He glanced over at Rasheed and tried to make eye contact, but his colleague was checking his phone at that moment, so he had no way of putting him on high alert.

And since he didn't see any other way of intervening, he let himself slide from his bar stool and approached the melee to try and make his way to Georgina to see why she had given him the bat signal. When he arrived at her seat, he saw that she was gone!

Christ—not again!

He glanced around frantically, and then he saw her: she was just leaving the club via the same back exit she had been taken through the night before, only this time at least under her own steam. He caught her eye and gave her a nod. The next moment, he was standing next to Rasheed and gave his colleague a tap on the shoulder. Rasheed looked up in alarm, and when Leland gestured in the direction of the exit, he immediately sprang into action.

They were only seconds behind Georgina, but even so, she had already moved out of sight. She couldn't be far, though, so he and Rasheed hurried to catch up with their colleague.

Hopefully, they'd find her before she did something reckless.

* * *

EVEN THOUGH GEORGINA remembered very little of what happened to her the night before, she hoped that by putting herself in the same position, something might be triggered and she would get a sudden flash of recollection. She had this vague notion that she must have caught a glimpse of the guy's face, but try as she might, the incident remained a big blur.

She was determined to catch this guy before he made more victims, which is why she was seated in the exact same place as the night before, only this time she wouldn't leave her drink unattended. As she sat there waiting, it gradually dawned on her that her theory was probably flawed, for no memories rushed back into her mind. Not like you saw in the movies sometimes, when the victim of a crime suddenly has this huge brainwave and she remembers exactly what her attacker looked like. But since she was too stubborn to admit defeat, she stayed glued to her spot, hoping that something would happen—anything—before she had to admit to Leland and Rasheed she'd dragged them out there for nothing.

The bartender was a different person from the night before and seemed more inclined to keep the glasses topped up. Several times she had to put her hand on her glass, or he would have filled it to the brim again. She wasn't there to get drunk. All she wanted was to…

And then suddenly, she saw it: the man standing next to her reached over to grab his drink, and she caught a glimpse of the tattoo on his wrist. It was a two-headed snake. And as she stared at the tattoo, suddenly her mind flashed back to an image of the same tattoo, this time on the wrist of the man who had dragged her out of the club last night. In trying to hold her up—for she was already mostly out of it—she had seen that very same tattoo.

It was him—it was her attacker!

CHAPTER 25

*L*eland and Rasheed had finally caught up with Georgina, and the three of them were in hot pursuit of the man she reckoned was her attacker. Though they didn't seem convinced.

"There are probably lots of people with a snake tattoo on their wrist," Leland argued.

"This one was a two-headed snake," she explained.

"I saw you last night, Georgina. You were completely out of it. This guy had to drag you along like a sack of potatoes."

She decided to give him a pass on the comparison. "I'm telling you it's him. I have a hunch."

"Usually it's Holt who has the hunches," Rasheed said. When she gave him a look of exasperation, he admitted, "I guess everyone is entitled to have hunches, not just the boss." He turned to Leland. "Do you recognize him? You got a good look last night, didn't you?"

"I'm not sure," said Leland, plucking at his hideous mustache. "It could be him."

She rolled her eyes. "Trust me, it's him. I have a—"

"Hunch. Yeah, you said," said Rasheed.

They had been following the guy for the past ten minutes, and so far so good. She didn't think he had detected that he was being followed. They had left the Marquee behind, and the nightlife area where all the clubs and bars were located, and were on their way to the old Leopold Barracks, which had recently been renovated and restored to their old glory.

The guy paused on a street corner, across the street from a well-known friterie. He lit up a cigarette and stood leaning against a tree, looking around intently.

Georgina and her colleagues stayed well out of sight and kept a close eye on the guy.

"Looks like he's waiting for someone," said Rasheed.

He was right. Five minutes later, a second man joined him, this one dressed in a hoodie and jeans. A plastic baggie and a bundle of cash changed hands, and both men went on their merry way. A drug deal, right under their noses.

"We should arrest him right now," said Leland.

"Let's see where he takes us," Georgina suggested. She didn't want to jump the gun. Even though they could arrest him for possession, she wanted him for the spiking. And since her own statement wouldn't suffice, they needed more. "Did you get all that?"

Rasheed held up his phone. "Got it," he confirmed.

The guy now seemed a lot more relaxed than he had been before. He crossed the street and walked into the friterie, texting on his phone all the while.

"You go," she told Rasheed. "You're the only one he hasn't seen yet."

"Medium one for me," said Leland, and he wasn't even joking.

They watched as Rasheed walked into the friterie after their suspect, and Georgina crossed her fingers that he wouldn't have clocked the detective at the Marquee. She didn't think he had, since Rasheed had kept well out of sight throughout.

"So you don't trust my mustache, huh?" said Leland, as he fingered the hideous thing. "Even though you said it altered my appearance to such an extent even my own mother wouldn't recognize me?"

"I just want to make sure we don't tip this guy off."

She waited impatiently for the suspect to walk out again, and it wasn't long until he did, carrying a large helping of fries with a heaping tower of mayonnaise on top. Then again, if he was indeed the rapist, he needed to keep his strength up.

Moments later Rasheed followed, not carrying anything.

"I didn't have time!" he said when Leland held up his hands in a gesture of exasperation. Ever so casually, the suspect started back in the direction of the Overpoort nightlife area, picking at his fries all the while. Finally, they had arrived back at the Marquee, and they watched him enter via the back door and disappear inside.

"What do we do?" asked Leland.

"We better keep an eye on that guy," said Georgina. "He might be targeting a new victim as we speak."

And so they split up, and one by one drifted into the club. But try as she might, Georgina couldn't locate the suspect again. Looked like he had managed to disappear. She searched the entire club—all three dance floors and six bars —and couldn't locate the guy at all.

Finally, she met up with Rasheed and Leland in the cloak-room at the front of the club. They both shrugged helplessly.

"Looks like he vanished into thin air," said Leland.

"But how! We all saw him walk in!" said Georgina, extremely frustrated that their quarry had managed to evade them.

"Maybe he walked in and immediately walked out again via the front?" Leland suggested.

Which would mean that he had known he was being followed and knew he had to shake them off.

"He didn't see us," said Rasheed. "Impossible. We kept out of sight the entire time."

He was right. He had never once given any indication that he was aware that he was being followed. If he had, he wouldn't have made that drug deal.

This was baffling, and extremely frustrating. But at least they had caught the guy's picture. They'd run it through the database and try to get a match.

"Maybe we can send it to the task force," Rasheed suggested. "It's possible that this guy is on their list of suspects already. They might even have his name on file."

"We can't do that," said Georgina. "If we did, Holt would know that we disobeyed a direct order." Holt had told them in no uncertain terms: no more adventures. Georgina had been lucky once, but who knows what could happen if she went after this guy again.

"Okay, I guess we better call it a night."

They'd been so close, and still had managed to lose the guy.

Talk about a frustrating end to a promising night.

"At least you didn't get attacked this time," said Leland as they started the trek home.

"Let's not do this again?" said Rasheed. "Leave things to the task force from now on?"

"I guess," said Georgina, though secretly she had a bad feeling about this task force. If they really wanted to nail this guy, why hadn't they been present at the Marquee the way they had? It was almost as if they didn't take this investigation seriously. Though if they had been present, they would have told Holt that three members of his team had been there, and that would have meant having to explain to him why they had decided to ignore his strict instructions to leave well enough alone.

CHAPTER 26

*W*ill Canavan imagined the look of pleasant surprise on his friend's face when he showed him the bottle. Usually, he got them the cheapest red he could find, but sometimes you got these crazy deals, and that's what he was grasping in his hot little hand right now: an excellent Beaujolais at the price of an Aldi store-brand wine. It was probably too early in the day for wine, but at least they could have a sip and save the rest for later in the day.

His trusty German Shepherd, Muppet, was way ahead of him and had already jumped aboard the barge. He knew the way, of course, as did Will. He'd been friends with Barney for years, ever since they were both living on the street—the two of them and Grady. They used to call themselves the Three Musketeers, with Grady being Porthos and Barney and Will the other two—whatever their names were.

Someone had once told him that there used to be four musketeers, but he didn't think that was correct. He remembered it as being three musketeers. But if people insisted, they could count Muppet as the fourth musketeer. Though Barney would probably argue that it was instead the stray that showed up at the barge from time to time. Will didn't care one way or the other. He was simply glad to still be alive, and so was Barney. The two of them had shared so many hardships that it was a miracle they were still on this side of the veil.

"Barney," he said as he managed to traverse the gangplank and make it safely to the other side without breaking a leg or another part of his anatomy. "Barney, you should see what I got. Deal of the century, brother. Deal of the millennium!"

But when he knocked on the door that led down into the barge's main cabin, there was no response. And that's when Muppet started to howl like crazy—he just raised his snout to the sky and produced this awful, terrible sound. Like a wolf on a full-moon night or something. Not that Will had ever heard an actual wolf howling, but he could imagine this was what it sounded like. It just went through him like a buzz-saw.

"Christ, knock it off, will you?" he grumbled.

He raised a shaking hand to the door handle and pressed down on it, then pushed his way into the cabin. And what he saw there was enough to curdle the blood in his veins. No wonder Muppet was howling!

There, on the carpet in front of the tiny TV set that Will had once picked up from MediaMarkt for no money at all, lay his best friend Barney, eyes speared open wide and his chest a bloody mess.

It didn't take more than two brain cells to determine that he was dead.

* * *

"WHO CALLED IT IN?" asked Holt.

"That guy over there," said the officer who had arrived first on the scene. "His name is Will Canavan, and he's a close friend of the victim. Says he was dropping off a bottle of red wine when he found him like that."

"Red wine?"

"Yeah, says he often dropped by for breakfast, and always brought a present."

"Must have been quite a shock," Holt said as he glanced over to Mr. Canavan, who seemed to bear up remarkably well, considering the circumstances.

"Yeah, it was a shock to me, too," said the officer, starting to become garrulous. "It's my first dead body," he explained. "I didn't expect there to be so much blood, sir. Blood everywhere," he added as he went a little pale at the recollection.

Holt patted him on the back. "You'll get used to it, son."

He stepped aboard the barge and watched as Tomas Lovelass walked out of the barge's living quarters, if that's what they were called. They probably had a special name, like everything else on a boat. Not that he cared much about terminology. A dead body is a dead body, wherever it is found.

"And? What do you think?" he asked.

"That whoever did this is some kind of animal," said the coroner. "Slashed his throat right open and then kept on stabbing, apparently for the sheer heck of it."

"So it was a human that did this?" he asked, just to make sure there were no misunderstandings.

"Oh, this was a human, all right," said Tomas. "No animal would take such enjoyment in the act of killing, I can tell you that."

"Time of death?"

"Hold on!" suddenly a voice shouted behind them. They both looked up, and Holt saw that Commissioner Terrence Bayton had arrived, with Roy Hesketh in tow and a couple of other detectives from the Ekkergem detective's department. They were approaching the gangplank. "This is my case now," Terrence bellowed from the quay. "So whatever you have to say, you better say it to me, Lovelass."

"God," Holt muttered.

"Not God," said Tomas with a grin. "Though he acts like it."

"Okay, looks like this case is out of my hands," said Holt. "There's one thing I forgot to ask you, Tomas. When we talked yesterday, I got the impression you weren't a big fan of Sebastian Kirkpatrick. Any particular reason?"

The coroner gave him a guarded look. "This isn't going on record, is it?"

"Not if you don't want it to."

"It's just that—as you probably must have guessed—I had a thing for Margo back in the day. And so when Sebastian suddenly popped up on the scene, I wasn't all that happy. Especially because he struck me as something of a poser, if you know what I mean. All flash and no substance. But Margo fell for his act hook, line, and sinker. And I lost my chance."

"If it makes you feel any better, he's still a poser," said Holt as he gave the other man's shoulder a pat. "Only these days he's a poser with a lot of money in his bank account."

Tomas flicked his wedding ring. "Don't feel bad for me, Holt. It took me a while, but I finally found the one. And my marriage is still going strong."

"Good for you," said Holt, and he meant it.

Terrence and his team had arrived, so it was time for him to skedaddle. "No more bricks through windows then?" he asked as Terrence joined him and Tomas.

"No more bricks," Terrence confirmed. "According to my information, this is just a random mugging," he told Holt. "No need for the feds to bother, so I'm taking over."

"Be my guest," said Holt. "It's a pretty nasty one, though. Don't say I didn't warn you."

The moment Terrence entered the small space, Holt could hear him make a retching sound. It elicited a grin from Roy, who gave Holt a wink. "Stomach not what it used to be."

CHAPTER 27

⚮

*W*hen Holt and Poppy arrived back at the office, he was satisfied to discover his team had already been hard at work. The first one to catch his attention was Leland.

"Boss, I checked the alibi of that fitness trainer guy, and turns out he was at the club, but not until eleven-thirty like he said. The woman he was with says she left at ten-thirty, when the club closed, and he walked out with her. She also said that he was extremely flirty, and seemed to have gotten it into his head that she was going home with him 'for a private session and some fun.' She told him in no uncertain terms that wasn't happening, and consequently canceled all of her future sessions with the guy."

"Looks like Mr. Cross's charm isn't as irresistible as he imagines," said Poppy.

"It also means that he lied to us about his alibi," said Holt. "You better go and pay him a visit, Leland. And try to impress upon him the consequences of lying to a police officer."

He still didn't think the man was capable of murder, but lying about his alibi certainly wasn't doing him any favors.

"Boss?" said Rasheed. "I've been going through Sebastian Kirkpatrick's financial statements and his business accounts. Looks like he hasn't been entirely honest with us either. Look who's a major investor in his nightclub empire."

Holt leaned over the desk and followed Rasheed's finger. "Well, I'll be damned," he said. "Ari Toropainen, aka The Atlas." He looked up at his daughter. "Looks like we'll be paying another visit to our grieving widower."

"Why does everyone think it's okay to lie to the police?" asked Georgina, voicing a grievance they all shared. "I mean, do they really think that's in their best interests?"

"I guess they don't think we'll find out," said Leland.

"They all think they're smarter than we are," said Poppy.

"Sometimes they are," said Rasheed. "I wouldn't want to know all the things that people keep from telling us. It probably would have saved us heaps of trouble."

"We'll just have to keep digging," said Holt. "And prove to them that we're not the dumbasses they take us for."

Georgina was right, though. Holt also hated it when he was being lied to. Which is why, when they finally were face to face with Mr. Kirkpatrick, he wasn't giving him the benefit of the doubt, as he had the first time they met.

"You lied to us, Mr. Kirkpatrick," he said, not beating around the bush. "You told us that you hadn't been in touch with your brother-in-law for years, and yet here we are, with him as one of your major investors. He's even on record as one of the co-owners of several of your clubs. How do you explain that?"

They were in the man's impressive living room again, where they had been the day before, only this time the businessman had a visitor, in the form of Ruby Floss. She had walked out of the kitchen when they walked in, and unfortunately her presence had a debilitating effect on Poppy, who couldn't stop staring at the pop singer—star-struck.

Miss Floss had decided to drape herself across the couch while they conducted the interview, and even though Holt had suggested she take a walk while they talked to Kirkpatrick, she hadn't taken the hint. And since Kirkpatrick didn't seem bothered by her presence, he couldn't very well kick her out since it was the nightclub owner's home.

"Look, I didn't lie to you," said Kirkpatrick as he leaned forward. "I haven't seen Ari in years. Okay, so he invested in my business. But he's a silent investor. He doesn't get involved with the day-to-day business of running the clubs. That's all me. He just provided me with some of the money to get started, mainly on Margo's instigation, who figured it would be a way for her brother to launch himself in business. But ever since he decided that being a gangster was more important to him than being a legit businessman, I'd much rather he let me buy him out. But he won't let me. He probably figures it's easy money."

"How do you know if you aren't in touch?"

"He uses a middleman. A lawyer. Like I said, I haven't spoken to or laid eyes on Ari since I got married to Margo."

"Was she still in touch with her brother?"

"I believe she was, yes. I told her it was a bad idea, but he was family, so she didn't want to cut him off."

"Do you know where we can find him?"

"No idea. For all I know he's in Dubai right now, living it up with his ill-gotten gains. Except for the money he made through me, of course," he added with a grin.

"Sebastian is telling you the truth, Chief Inspector," said Ruby now. "He's the most honest person I know. If he tells you that he hasn't seen his brother-in-law, he hasn't seen him." She gave the man a fond look. "And I should know, since I've known Seb forever."

"He used to be your manager, didn't he?" asked Poppy.

"That's right," said Ruby. "My first manager, and probably the best of the lot. I should have stuck with him, but you know how it goes. I was young and ambitious and figured I could do better. It has taken me all this time to discover that there are plenty of sharks out there and very few honest people."

"That's so sweet of you to say," said Sebastian coyly. "To be absolutely honest, I didn't have a clue what it meant to be a manager. I was making it up as I went along, you know."

"You were still better than half of the so-called professionals out there," said the famous singer. "At least you didn't try to steal my money, like most of them do."

"I always tried to do right by you," said Sebastian, continuing the string of reminiscences that Holt wasn't all that interested in. But when he saw that his daughter was listening intently, her cheeks and ears bright red, he figured it wouldn't hurt to stick around a little while longer. How often do you get the chance to talk to a world-famous star?

"I heard that you had to cancel your tour," asked Poppy. "I hope you're not... I mean I hope you're all right?"

"Oh, I'm fine," Ruby assured her. "But it's very sweet of you to ask. I'm having some trouble with my voice." She coughed. "You can probably hear it. I've been a little hoarse lately, and the prospect of going on stage every night just isn't in the cards right now."

"She's seeing a throat doctor, aren't you, darling?"

"Yeah, he's amazing. I'm hoping that he can fix me." She laughed. "Fix me—that doesn't sound right!"

"He will fix your voice," Sebastian assured her. "Just you wait and see. He's the best," he told them. "The best of the best."

"Like you," said Ruby as she grasped Sebastian's hand and gave it a squeeze. "And since wherever I go I'm being hounded by the media and the fans these days, Seb has invited me to stay with him while I see this doctor. Back to my roots, so to speak."

"Anything I can do to help, darling."

Before the lovebirding got out of hand, Holt decided to leave. Poppy didn't seem inclined to, but he felt they'd probably outstayed their welcome. And so they said their goodbyes, and as Sebastian escorted them to the door, the man lowered his voice and asked, "You really think Ari killed Margo?"

"We don't," Holt said. "But we can't rule it out either. Which is why we need to find him, so we can cross him off our list of suspects. So if Ari does get in touch with you..."

Sebastian nodded. "I'll talk to his lawyer. Tell him to cooperate. Though I hope to God he wasn't the one that did this to Margo. I mean, I know he's a gangster and all, but she was his sister, for crying out loud."

"Unfortunately, to people like Ari, things like a familial bond don't always matter as much as they do to us," said Poppy. She cut a quick glance in the direction of the living room, where the idol of her youth still lounged, but then managed to tear herself away and followed Holt out.

CHAPTER 28

*G*eorgina couldn't let it go. Even though Leland had told her not to pursue the matter and hand it over to the task force, she just couldn't do it. Instead, she had sent the pictures to a friend on the drug squad, to try and get a name for the drug dealer that their suspect had met last night, and maybe, if they were lucky, also for the suspect himself.

"Bingo!" she said as she hung up. "Guess what? Our friendly neighborhood drug dealer has been identified. His name is Bradford Brewer and he's been on their radar."

"Did your friend also know who Brewer's client was?" asked Leland.

Georgina's excitement waned a little. "No, she didn't. But she did reveal that Brewer is affiliated with The Atlas's network. Not sure if that's relevant, but I thought it might be."

"We have to tell Holt," said Leland. "Especially with this new information that's come to light. If he finds out we've been going around his back, he won't be best pleased."

"I know. But if we do tell him, he'll be livid. You know how he hates dishonesty."

"So what do you suggest?"

"Let me try and ID this guy, and then we'll tell him, all right? At least then he'll have a result on his desk." Holt might hate dishonesty, but he loved to nab a perp even more. So if they could collar this guy, he'd forgive them for going behind his back. Leland didn't look convinced. "Don't tell him, Leland. I swear to God, if you do, I'll wring your neck."

"I won't tell him!" Leland cried, holding up his hands. "But you better get a result soon. The suspense is killing me!"

It was killing her even more. But she'd started down this road and couldn't turn back now. She had to see this through, no matter what.

* * *

RASHEED KEPT his head down and his nose glued to the computer monitor. He hated this. He hated having to lie to his boss, and he couldn't imagine this would end well. Holt was a great boss. He'd managed, through some kind of miracle, to get them all promoted from a sleepy backwater local police department to being in the middle of where the action was, and they should all be eternally grateful to the man, who was as loyal as they came. And this was how Georgina was repaying him? This was so wrong on so many levels.

He was actually considering going behind Georgina and Leland's backs and telling Holt the truth. Or maybe tell Poppy, so she could break the bad news and cushion the blow.

To be honest, he didn't know what to do, and so he did the only thing he could think of: continue running the image of that guy through the database and hoping he'd get a match.

The moment they did, they could sell the result to Holt—he was sure of it.

Now if only he could find out who this mystery man was…

* * *

THE CALL that Holt had been waiting for had finally come: permission to talk to Clarissa McMinn. Apparently, the doctor in charge of her recovery had seen it fit to grant them access to the woman. And so Poppy parked the car in front of the clinic and hoped that the woman would be compos mentis and would be able to give them a clue as to what had happened to her husband.

Admittedly, they had been distracted by the murder of Margo Kirkpatrick and hadn't paid as much attention to finding the missing plastic surgeon, but that couldn't be helped. At least they'd put in some hours on that particular case, with their nocturnal stake-outs, that so far had yielded nothing.

"Do you still think that The Atlas was behind McMinn's abduction?" she asked as she tried to keep up with her dad. "Only if he's got nothing to do with it, we're wasting our time staking out the guy's clinic."

To be honest, she was starting to feel the strain of spending half the night staking out the guy's place and spending the day working a regular shift. But since resources were stretched thin, as they always were, there was no second team that could take over the investigation.

"It seems plausible," said her dad as he held open the door for her. "The guy needs a new face but can't do it openly, as he would be arrested before he's on the operating table. And here's this plastic surgeon with a stellar reputation being kidnapped in broad daylight, gangster style. I think this is still our best shot at finding Dr. McMinn."

Once again, they couldn't get past Dr. Shawn Luukkonen, who was acting as gatekeeper, same as last time. Only instead of telling them in mournful tones that he couldn't allow them to speak to his patient, this time he was the bearer of glad tidings of joy. "She's made a remarkable recovery," he announced when they met him in reception. Only this time, he walked them through to the wing where presumably his patient was being housed. "I'm always amazed and humbled to witness the resilience of the human spirit, and I think it's safe to say that's on full display here."

"Will she be able to leave soon?" asked Poppy, who didn't like this guy at all. If he was a friend of Clarissa's husband and had conspired to have her locked up, he was nothing more than a common criminal. She just wished she could arrest him now and lock *him* up.

The doctor pursed his lips. "If she keeps up this rate of recovery, I don't see why not. Though not for another couple of weeks."

"Weeks?"

"Or months. We don't want to discharge her before she is ready to face the world again. The worst thing that could happen is a relapse. I wouldn't want that on my conscience."

She opened her mouth to say something particularly poignant yet scathing about the guy's conscience, but Holt stopped her with a gesture of his hand.

He was probably right. They didn't want to antagonize the man before they'd spoken to his patient.

They had passed several doors, and at a lot of them, the doctor had to apply his badge to grant them access. This place had more security than a prison. Finally, they arrived at the wing where the most challenging patients were being kept: the ones that had been committed against their will.

Security was tight, with several burly orderlies on standby to make sure no funny business occurred on their watch.

They were led into a large room where several patients sat playing games or otherwise stared in front of them, looking rather forlorn. Poppy felt for them and could only imagine this was probably what hell looked like. For a moment, she experienced a sense of panic that this doctor would lock them both up here, but then she dismissed the thought. He would never do a crazy thing like that. Or would he?

"And this is Clarissa," said Doctor Luukkonen as he placed his hands on the back of a chair. On the chair, a slender woman was seated. Her face was extremely pale, and her mousy brown hair hung limply around that same face like an unwashed curtain.

"These are police detectives, Clarissa," said the doctor, enunciating clearly. "They want to ask you a couple of questions about Sandy. Think you're up for that?"

Clarissa glanced up at them with a pair of pale blue eyes and nodded. "Yes, doctor."

"Good," said the doctor. "Excellent." He gave the two detectives a smile. "Well, I'll leave you to it. Let's say twenty minutes? We don't want to tire her too much."

He patted Clarissa's shoulder and left. Now it was just the three of them—and a room filled with other patients.

CHAPTER 29

The first thing Poppy noticed was that the woman wasn't as mentally challenged as she'd been made out to be. Sure, she looked like hell warmed over, but when they started talking, she answered all of their questions without hesitation.

"Yeah, I had some kind of breakdown, I guess you could call it," she explained. "Not sure what brought it on. One morning I just didn't want to get up. I wanted to stay in bed forever, and not bother with getting ready for work and dropping Tommy off at the daycare and then doing the crazy commute, braving traffic, my psychopath boss and my sycophantic colleagues."

"What do you do for a living?" asked Poppy.

"HMO. I know it's a little ironic, considering my husband is a doctor. We used to joke we were on opposite sides of the fence. Usually, it's fine, and there's some excellent benefits, like the daycare is run by my employer, and also the cleaning service we use, and we get a discount. But lately..." She shook her head, her tawdry tresses dangling listlessly around her head. "We got a new boss, and she's super critical of everything I do. Weekly performance reviews. I swear, she's just looking for a reason to get rid of me. I used to enjoy going to work, but now it's just a drag. I've been thinking of chucking it in, but that's exactly what she wants, and I don't want to give her the satisfaction." She gave them a weak smile. "Anyway, you didn't come all the way out here to hear me complain about my boss."

"The thing is, Clarissa," said Holt, "I don't know if anyone has told you this, but your husband has been abducted."

"I know," she said. "My sister told me."

"Your sister was allowed to talk to you?"

"Oh, sure. She's been in every day since I was admitted."

Holt shared a look with Poppy. Odd that they hadn't been allowed to pay Clarissa a visit and her sister had. Then again, they were cops, and her sister was, well, her sister.

"Any idea where he might be?" asked Clarissa.

"Not yet," said Holt. "We're out looking for him, though."

She didn't seem all that broken up about her husband going missing. "You wouldn't have any idea who took him?" asked Poppy.

"No idea," said the woman. She squeezed her eyebrows together. "I'm worried about Tommy. My sister told me that he was in the car with his dad when he was taken?"

"Yes, but he's fine," said Poppy. "Your sister is taking care of him."

"Oh, I know," said Clarissa. "She told me. If it wasn't for her, I probably would have busted down the doors to get out of here. And I have to say the whole thing has given me the motivation to get better as soon as I can. So I can see my boy again."

Poppy noticed how she didn't mention her husband. And so even though she probably shouldn't, she felt she should bring up the difficult topic. "Your sister seems to feel that your husband shouldn't have had you committed."

"Yeah, I know. Wanda has never been a big fan of Sandy. She wore all black when we got married, as a sign of mourning. Sandy wasn't amused. But I don't think he'd have me committed. He did it because this is a great hospital and he knows the head doctor."

"Is it true that you're considering a divorce?" asked Holt.

"Yeah, that's true. Though now I'm not so sure. I think I said that because I was feeling so low. It wasn't Sandy's fault that I was feeling as bad as I was. I took it out on him, and that wasn't fair on my part. I see that now. So I'm not going to make a decision until I feel like I've put this behind me." She took a deep breath. "I'm determined to give our marriage another try. I haven't been a good wife to Sandy."

"Well…" said Poppy, but caught her dad's eye and shut up again. She would have told the woman not to be gaslighted by her husband and his doctor friend, but frankly speaking, what did she know? Maybe Clarissa was right and she simply needed a break from her life to try and get well again.

"You will find Sandy, won't you?" asked Clarissa.

"We will find him," Holt assured her.

Poppy didn't share his confidence. If the gangsters that took him meant business, they might find him with his throat slit. Though she wasn't going to tell the woman that, of course.

"The name Ari Toropainen, does that ring a bell to you?" asked Holt. "Also known as The Atlas?"

Clarissa frowned. "Is this in connection with the abduction of my husband?" When Holt nodded, she shook her head. "I don't think I've ever heard Sandy mention that name, no. Though to be honest, he doesn't discuss his patients with me. He takes confidentiality very seriously, and would never betray a patient's confidence."

After they had taken their leave, Poppy fumed, "The guy is totally gaslighting her! Making her feel as if it's all her fault and he's just doing this to save her! When all the while he's the one who had her committed because she was talking divorce!"

"We don't know that, Poppy," said Holt. "For all we know, he did it from the best motives and really loves his wife. We won't know until we talk to him. But first we have to find him."

"I still think he's a no-good piece of—"

They almost bumped into Doctor Luukkonen, who seemed pleased to see them. "And? How did it go?" he asked.

"She was extremely lucid," said Holt.

"Yes, like I said, she had a sudden breakthrough and has been doing a lot better. I think this abduction may be the impetus she needs to fight her way back. Especially the fact that her son is now without both his parents." He held out his hand. "Goodbye, chief inspector."

"Thank you, doctor," said Holt, pressing the man's hand.

"Please let me know if there's any development," he said as he walked on. "And I'll be sure to pass it on to my patient."

"His patient," Poppy scoffed. "His prisoner more likely."

She probably should have kept her voice down, for when she happened to glance over her shoulder, she saw that Doctor Luukkonen was giving her a very dirty look indeed.

CHAPTER 30

*R*asheed stared at his screen. He almost couldn't believe it, but he'd finally gotten a hit on the picture of Georgina's wannabe rapist. The young man staring back at him definitely shared some of the features of the man they had seen last night. His eyes were the same color, for one thing, though in his mugshot he was a lot younger, and suffered from quite a severe case of acne. His hair color was also different. He'd been dark-haired back then, and blond now. Was it the same man? He wasn't sure. Maybe the others would know.

"Georgina—Leland!" he said, leaning back. "I got a hit."

His colleagues immediately came over to check.

"Yep, that's him," said Georgina. "I'd recognize that ugly mug anywhere."

"He's not exactly ugly, though, is he?" said Leland. When Georgina gave him a scathing look, he amended, "Okay, so he's not handsome either."

"I guess he's not bad-looking," Georgina admitted. "But it's in his eyes. You can see the evil in his eyes."

Rasheed didn't see any evil in the guy's eyes, but then

maybe you had to have a special sixth sense to see it. What he did see was the guy's rap sheet, which told him they'd been lucky. The guy had only been arrested once, for possession and the illegal distribution of drugs as a teenager. If he'd never been arrested, they'd never have been able to get a hit.

"Do you want to tell Holt, or should I?" asked Rasheed, feeling that now was the time to broach this difficult subject.

Leland and Georgina shared a look. "I guess I better tell him," said Georgina. "After all, it was my idea to go after this guy."

"When we show him the result, he'll be glad that you did," said Leland.

Rasheed wasn't all that convinced. He didn't share Georgina's conviction that this was the same guy from last night. Even though the computer had spat out a positive result, that didn't mean anything. Probably it was a good idea to let Holt decide what to do.

* * *

POPPY HAD ASKED her dad to drop her off at home. Her new home. He'd brought over some more of her stuff from Loveringem, and she was going to drop it off at the place she and Bernard now shared. She hadn't officially moved in—for one thing, her official address was still listed as Loveringem —but she was getting there. She liked to move slow, remembering how devastated she had been when she discovered that her previous boyfriend had cheated on her with an influencer-slash-model. This time she wasn't taking any chances and was moving at a snail's pace. Bernard would have to prove himself, but so far the signs were good. In fact the only person who didn't seem to approve of Bernard was her dad, but then he had always been overly protective of her and extremely critical of any boyfriend she introduced.

In that sense, he was simply following his own instinct as a dad.

Holt took off again in the direction of the precinct while she entered the apartment building—Bernard had given her her own key a couple of weeks after they first started dating. She lugged her heavy duffel bag into the elevator and allowed it to swish her up to the fourth floor where Bernard's apartment was located. He didn't actually own it outright but was simply renting it. She had already suggested that she pay her share of the rent, but so far he had graciously declined. Once she moved in officially, she would insist, though.

She stuck her key in the door and tiptoed into the apartment, knowing to be as quiet as a mouse since Bernard most likely was asleep in the bedroom. He usually slept with earplugs and the heavy curtains drawn. Otherwise, he'd never be able to sleep.

She placed her bag on the floor and looked around. The place lacked that je ne sais quoi that made it feel like a true home. Maybe some art on the walls, different furniture arrangement—or different furniture altogether. And she hated—*hated*—the wall color, which was a dark gray and quite depressing. It had been like this when Bernard moved in, and he hadn't bothered to put his personal touch on the place, figuring he wouldn't be there long.

He'd been dreaming of buying his own place, but even though he made good money at the club, it wasn't enough to be able to put up a down payment for an actual house.

Maybe the two of them, when they combined their salaries, would be able to convince the bank to offer them a loan at a reasonable interest rate. But they weren't at that stage yet. Easy does it was her motto, and definitely when it came to buying a house together.

Maybe some of her dad's carefulness had rubbed off on her after all.

She walked into the spare bedroom, which Bernard had been using as storage space, and looked out across the back-yards of the other houses on the block. Beyond that was a school, and she could hear and see the kids playing. She smiled. Maybe one day she and Bernard would have kids, and they'd go to that school. Now wouldn't that be something?

She sat down on top of the desk that had been positioned flush with the windowsill, and as she let her mind idly spin out scenarios for a possible future for her and Bernard, she noticed a small leather pouch that she'd never seen before. It was lying on the desk, and looked like a pencil case. Curious, she opened it and was surprised to find different small plastic bags containing pills. There were white pills, but also pills of every possible color.

There was also a small vial containing a clear liquid, and for some reason, a syringe.

She took out the syringe and held it up to the light, wondering if Bernard was diabetic and hadn't told her. But if he was, she probably would have noticed, wouldn't she?

She took out one of the baggies containing multi-colored pills and let a few of them roll into the palm of her hand. Her heart plummeted in her chest. She might not know what was in the syringe, but she knew exactly what these pills were.

Drugs.

And just as she picked up another baggie, this one containing white pills, there was a rustling sound behind her. When she turned around, she found herself face to face with Bernard.

He was shaking his head, a sad look in his eyes.

"I so wish you hadn't seen that, Poppy."

CHAPTER 31

*W*hen Holt arrived, he didn't even have time to aim his coat at the coatrack. Georgina came walking straight up to him. Behind her, both Rasheed and Leland directed curious looks in his direction, and he immediately knew they'd been up to something—again.

He sighed. "Okay, what is it this time?"

"Well, the thing is, boss," said Georgina. "Remember you told me to drop the investigation into those spikings?"

"And leave it to the task force? Yes, I remember that very well." He arched an eyebrow. "You didn't drop it?"

She shook her head. "Not… exactly."

"We got him, boss," said Leland. "We got the guy."

"What do you mean, you got the guy?" he asked, tamping down the temptation to give these three a good dressing-down and a speech about the importance of following orders. Then again, they were good cops, and wasn't he the epitome of insubordination? He was the one who had knocked out his superior officer that time. Not exactly a shining example.

"Okay, so we returned to the Marquee last night," said

Georgina, her eyes not wavering from his—gauging his response to her words. He simply stared at her. "And I recognized the guy who spiked me. I mean, I suddenly remembered that he had a tattoo of a two-headed snake on his wrist. And so when I saw one of the men at the bar with a similar tattoo, I figured he might be the one."

An uncomfortable feeling suddenly assaulted Holt. "You're saying your attacker had a tattoo of a snake on his wrist?"

Georgina nodded. "I had completely forgotten about it. It was only when I was at the Marquee, in the exact same location and circumstances, that the memory resurfaced."

"It's known as context-dependent memory," said Rasheed helpfully. "You can use it to jog your recollection of an event."

"So we followed the guy and saw him buy drugs from a street dealer," Georgina continued her story.

"A street dealer who works for The Atlas, by the way," Leland added. Now that his boss hadn't exploded, he was gaining confidence that their rogue mission would be seen as a success story and not the act of insubordination it could be construed as.

"And then he walked right back to the club and disappeared."

"We think he may have gone in through the back and left through the front," said Rasheed.

"Wait, you were also there?" asked Holt.

The three of them nodded guiltily. "I couldn't let her go out there on her own, boss," said Leland.

"I felt the same way," said Rasheed. "We weren't going to let this guy try and attack her again. And so we kept a close eye on him the whole time. Well, until he gave us the slip."

"But we took pictures," said Georgina. "And Rasheed has managed to get a positive ID."

That queasy feeling in his stomach wasn't abating but

getting stronger by the minute. And when Rasheed turned his computer screen and he got his first good look at 'the spiker,' it was as if the bottom fell out of his world.

"Oh, God," he muttered.

"Do you recognize him, boss?" asked Leland eagerly.

He nodded. "I do. That's Bernard."

Rasheed checked the screen. "Hey, you're right, boss. Bernard, um, Farre." He looked up. "Do you know him?"

"I do, yeah. He's Poppy's new boyfriend."

* * *

"I DON'T UNDERSTAND," said Poppy, even though she understood full well what was going on. Her dad had been right, as usual, and her own radar had malfunctioned disastrously.

Bernard dragged a hand through his shaggy blond mane. "It's my fault. I should never have started dating a cop. I just figured it was a lark, you know. You being a cop and me being…"

"A criminal?"

His eyes flashed dangerously, and she realized that she didn't know this man at all. "I've done my time, Poppy. I've paid my dues. No more arrests for the last seven years. I'm not the person I used to be back then."

"You've been in jail?"

"Like I said, I paid my dues. I don't think it's fair to hold a person responsible for stuff he did when he was just a kid. But knowing how a cop's mind works, I'm not surprised."

"Is that why you didn't tell me?"

"Of course!" he suddenly burst out. "Because I knew this would happen. I knew you'd end up turning against me."

"I'm not turning against you," she said as she slid off the desk. She was in a distinctly disadvantageous position, cornered and with her only route of escape cut off by Bernard.

"Yes, you are! You *and* your dad! Don't you think I know how he feels about me? He knows, Poppy. He knows what I did, and he'll hold it over me forever!"

"My dad hasn't done a background check on you, Bernard. So if you have a criminal record, he isn't aware of it."

"He probably didn't want to tell you," he said as he glowered at her. "Still trying to protect his little girl."

He was trying to get a rise out of her, but she wasn't going to allow herself to be distracted from her only goal right now: to get past this man somehow. Then again, he had never struck her as a violent person, and she found it hard to believe he would hurt her.

But since she was starting to see that she couldn't trust her own judgment, it was better to be safe than sorry.

"What about this?" she asked, gesturing to the pouch filled with drug paraphernalia.

"Oh, that," he said, with a throwaway gesture of his hand. "I'm just holding on to that for a friend. It's not mine."

"What about the syringe? Are you also holding on to that for a friend?" She probably shouldn't push him, but then again, she wanted some answers from this man.

"Absolutely," he said, nodding. "Look, you know how it is. You spend some time in jail, and you meet a lot of people that otherwise you would never, ever make the acquaintance of. And so I made some friends in prison that are still friends to this day."

"Friends with a drug habit."

"They're trying to get clean, but it's not easy, you know."

"Are you a drug addict, Bernard?"

"No, absolutely not!" he said. She had to admit that she had never seen any needle marks on his arms, or signs of an addiction, so she was inclined to believe him. He was holding out his hands now, palms up, and his arms were clean. The only thing that marred the smooth skin was a tattoo of a two-headed snake on his right wrist.

"Look, I know I probably should have told you," said Bernard. "But I knew you'd be obliged to turn me in, and so to protect my friend, I didn't. I hope you can forgive me, Poppy."

"You're right," she said. "You should have told me what was going on."

"Look, if you want, I'll get rid of all of this stuff," he suggested. "I'll throw it all away."

"Your friend won't like that."

"I don't care! You are more important to me than this friendship."

Was he telling the truth? He seemed genuine enough.

"I just don't want this stuff in our home, Bernard."

"I agree! Like I said, I'll get rid of it. I'll do it now," he said as he held out his hand.

She hesitated as she picked up the pouch. Every instinct told her that she shouldn't agree with this. She should tell her dad. She was a cop, for crying out loud. She couldn't just…

"Bernard," she said as she looked up at him.

She saw there was a strange gleam in his eyes. "You're going to have me arrested, aren't you? You cops are all the same. You simply can't help yourselves. Even though I told you I'm only doing a small service for a friend, you still can't let it slide this one time."

He was right. She couldn't turn a blind eye. She simply couldn't.

"Just let me call my dad. We'll explain it to him. Together."

But Bernard was shaking his head. "No way."

"We'll tell him what you just told me. I promise you he'll understand."

But as she watched his expression darken, she suddenly understood.

"There is no friend, is there? This stuff... it's all yours. *You* are the addict."

Before she could stop him, he had snatched the pouch from her hand and picked out the syringe. Dropping the pouch, he lunged for her, wielding the syringe like a knife. She ducked, and as she did, he narrowly missed plunging that syringe into her neck.

Trying to get past him, instead she slipped on the floor and went down hard.

Seeing that he had the advantage, he came at her again. So she kicked out as hard as she could with her booted foot. She hit him in the leg, which gave out from under him. This time he was the one who went down, and as he did, he accidentally injected himself with the syringe. The plunger was pressed all the way to the hilt, and whatever had been in that syringe was pumped into his system.

His eyes went wide when he realized what he'd done.

"Don't tell your dad," he said, which was an odd thing to say.

"You're crazy," she said as she scrambled to her feet. "What was in that syringe?"

He smiled and yanked out the syringe, but instead of getting up off the floor, he just sat there, almost as if whatever he'd injected himself with had somehow incapacitated him.

His eyes were starting to close, and a grin spread across his face. "I knew this was a bad idea," he said, his speech sounding slurred. He gestured between them. "You and me. The beauty and the beast." He closed his eyes and seemed to have trouble staying conscious.

"Bernard?" she said and cautiously approached him. She kicked the syringe away, and it skittered across the floor and underneath the desk. "Bernard, what was in that thing?"

She shook his shoulder, and he opened his eyes with some effort. "GHB," he said, but then his head lolled to the side, and he was out.

She sat back and studied him for a moment. And that's when the awful truth suddenly hit her. GHB. The date rape drug.

Suddenly her phone buzzed in her pocket, and she took it out. It was her dad, and she immediately picked up.

"Thank God!" he breathed into her ear. "Where are you?"

"At Bernard's place. Dad, I think you better get over here."

"I have some terrible news for you, honey." And as she listened to him explain how Georgina had identified Bernard as the man who had spiked her drink that night, her stomach turned, and she was suddenly violently sick.

She only managed to reach the bathroom just in time.

CHAPTER 32

*H*olt had wanted to skip their nightly stakeout of the surgeon's clinic, but Poppy had insisted they go. When he discovered that his daughter's boyfriend was the rapist, he had immediately sprung into action. He and his team hurried to Bernard's place to make the arrest—and to save Poppy from possible harm.

When they got there, Poppy had already incapacitated the guy, who was unconscious on the floor. Looked like he'd been served a dish of his own making.

Poppy had been devastated but had still managed to handle herself exemplarily in the face of the extremely shocking discovery that her boyfriend was a rapist and had possibly victimized dozens of people.

The task force had arrived and was going through his apartment with a fine-tooth comb. Undoubtedly, they would find more evidence linking him to a host of crimes.

Not for the first time in his life, Holt didn't know what to say.

They were sitting side by side, parked across the street from the clinic, and so far, nothing was happening. Poppy had picked up two bags of French fries and was eating them slowly, none of her usual relish on display—which was understandable.

Finally, Holt felt they should have the conversation.

He cleared his throat, but before he could launch into the speech he had carefully prepared in his head over the past couple of hours, she interrupted him by holding up a hand.

"I know what you're going to say, Dad, and you're absolutely right. I should have listened to you. Obviously, you're a much better judge of character than I am."

"That wasn't what I was going to say," he said.

She looked over. "Oh? Then what was it?"

Once again, he cleared his throat. He might be an excellent cop, but expressing his feelings had always been a foreign thing to him—something Leah had often faulted him for.

"First, I wanted to tell you how proud I am of the way you handled yourself back there. The way you managed to take Bernard out before he could do you any harm." He didn't mention how horrified he had been when she gave a blow-by-blow account of how the scene had played out. If Bernard had managed to plunge that syringe into her, who knows what he might have done to her.

"And secondly, I can't even begin to say how sorry I am that you found yourself in that situation. I should..." His voice broke. "This is all on me, honey. I should have known that he was bad news. And I should have done a background check on him."

"*I* should have done a background check on him," said Poppy. "Then I would have known what kind of guy he was. The only reason I didn't was that I didn't want to be the kind of person who does a background check on her boyfriend."

"Same here," he said quietly as he picked another fry from

his bag. For some reason, they didn't taste as good as they had the day before. As if they turned to ashes in his mouth.

"Look, you don't have anything to blame yourself for, Dad," she said. "This is all on me. You told me that you weren't convinced moving in with Bernard was a good idea, and you were right. Obviously, you were right about him, and I was wrong." She shook her head. "I'm such a lousy judge of character, it's hard to believe."

"No, you're not, honey. You just want to see the good in people all the time, and that's an admirable quality."

"Not so admirable when you end up moving in with a serial rapist and drug addict," she said as she slid deeper into her seat.

"You couldn't have known. Nobody knew. Not even the people he worked for."

"Sebastian Kirkpatrick," she said. She shared a quick look with her dad. "Odd that he wouldn't have launched his own investigation when the complaints started coming in."

"You think he knew and didn't stop Bernard?"

She shrugged. "I don't know. I just feel he could have done more to protect his customers. Almost as if he didn't care that he had a rapist on the loose in his clubs."

"I guess," said Holt as he picked another fry from his bag. He was staring out through the windshield at the clinic, but so far, nothing stirred. Looked like his hunch wasn't playing out the way he hoped. Maybe those rumors Rasheed had picked up were wrong, and The Atlas had nothing to do with the doctor's kidnapping? In which case, they were wasting their time.

"I should have made the link, you know," he said. "Who better to spike a person's drink than the bartender serving that drink?"

Though Bernard hadn't been on duty the night that Georgina was spiked, or her friend Jeanine. But he definitely knew the lay of the land. What they needed to figure out was whether he had worked alone or if some of the other bartenders were in on it with him.

"Can we talk about something else?" asked Poppy in a pained voice. "Like the investigation?"

"Of course," he said. He could understand her reluctance to hear another word about her ex-boyfriend's extracurricular activities. "What do you want to talk about?"

"Okay, so I think by now we've established that you have a pretty good gut feeling about people?"

"I guess." Though if he really did have such a great gut feeling, he would have looked deeper into Bernard when the idea first occurred to him.

"So let's go over the list of suspects in the Margo Kirkpatrick case, shall we?" She counted them on her fingers. "So far we have Sebastian Kirkpatrick."

"Motive?"

"He discovered that his wife was having an affair and decided to get rid of her. Though as far as we can tell, his alibi checked out. He was at that club when he said he was."

"Plus, he didn't have to kill her. He could have just gotten a divorce," he pointed out.

"Okay, then there's the lover. Orvo Cross. No alibi—something he lied about. And she was eager to move things to the next level, something he wasn't on board with."

"Same thing. He could have simply broken up with her."

Leland had another chat with the guy, and he claimed he'd simply been confused about the exact time he left the gym that night. Instead he'd gone home to bed. So no alibi.

"Then there's Terrence," said Poppy, tapping out her middle finger. "If what The Atlas claims is true, the police could have killed his sister to draw him out and make an arrest."

"You know I'm not exactly Terrence's biggest fan," said

Holt. "But even I don't think he's capable of doing something like that. And besides, there's no telling that ruse would have worked. The Atlas could skip his sister's funeral if he smelled a rat."

"Yeah, I guess that is unlikely. Terrence may color outside of the lines from time to time, but not even he would murder a woman just so he can arrest her brother." She sighed deeply. "So who else is there?"

"The Atlas's enemies? They could have decided that when they couldn't get to him, they might as well strike at his family?"

"As a way to put pressure on him, you mean? It's possible. I mean, in the milieu The Atlas operates in, one murder more or less is probably nothing. They could have kept a close eye on her and decided to strike when she was out jogging, the way she did every night. Too bad no one saw what happened —apart from that one witness who heard that scream. I mean, the canal is lined with barges, and most of them are inhabited."

"That barge," he said thoughtfully. "Funny you should say that. The guy who was murdered on his barge. Terrence figures it was a robbery gone wrong, but that barge is very close to the crime scene. Could it be that the man on the boat saw what happened?"

"And that the killer came back to get rid of him?"

"I mean, it's possible. By all accounts, Barney Waller wasn't a wealthy man. He didn't have anything worth stealing, and as far as I could tell, nothing of value *was* stolen." He shook his head. "I should have never allowed Terrence to muscle me out of that inquiry."

Just then, Poppy sat up with a jerk. "Dad!" she said, placing a hand on his arm. "I think this is it. I think it's finally happening!"

She was right. Across the street, a black van had drawn up

in front of the clinic, and a burly guy with sunglasses and a leather jacket had stepped out, scanning the street carefully before he tapped the side of the van. The door slid open and two more men stepped out, escorting a third man who looked very much like Sandy McMinn. As they led him up to the front door of the clinic, finally a tall guy stepped out of the van and buttoned up his jacket as he glanced around.

The bald head, the large port-wine stain on his face, the powerful build.

It was unmistakable: this was The Atlas!

$\mathcal{P}$oppy's dad knew better than to try and arrest The Atlas himself, and so the moment they had positively identified both the gangster and the plastic surgeon he had abducted, he called in backup. It wasn't long before a heavily armed POSA unit—Belgian SWAT— arrived and expertly took down The Atlas and his cronies. The driver and the other men escorting the prisoner didn't put up much of a resistance when they realized they were outmanned and outgunned. The only person who resisted arrest was The Atlas himself, and so it was a battered and bruised Ari Toropainen who was placed under arrest and transferred to the police station jail.

First, Holt and Poppy interviewed Dr. McMinn. All in all, the man didn't appear to have suffered adverse effects during his incarceration. He also admitted that he'd been treated with respect and consideration.

"All he wanted was to get rid of that port-wine stain," said the well-renowned plastic surgeon. He may have been treated well, but the abduction had clearly taken a toll on him, as he looked gaunt and tired, with purple circles under his eyes and a face the color of vomit. "He'd been suffering abuse because of the way he looks for so many years he was finally done with it. Only, he was a wanted man, and so he couldn't simply walk into my office and schedule the procedure. So instead he came up with the brilliant idea to stage my abduction and force me to operate on his face."

"Wasn't he afraid of getting caught when he used your clinic?" asked Holt.

They weren't in one of the interview rooms but in the conference room they used for visitors or if they wanted to talk to a victim or witness in private.

"I told him that my clinic was probably being watched, but he said the cops had no idea that he was behind my abduction. I knew better than to try and argue with the man. He treated me well, but I didn't have any illusions about the nature of our relationship. It wasn't a patient-doctor relationship but abductor-prisoner, and so I could never be at ease."

"Why did he decide to get rid of that stain now? I mean, he's been walking around with that thing all his life."

The surgeon shrugged. "You'd have to ask him. He didn't exactly confide in me. Normally we do an evaluation of the patient's psychological state before we engage in such a deeply invasive procedure, but in this case, that wasn't a possibility."

"There's one other thing I wanted to discuss with you, doctor," said Holt. "Your wife has been admitted to your friend Shawn Luukkonen's psychiatric hospital. We talked to several people, and there seems to be this persistent story that the only reason you had her admitted is because she was threatening you with divorce." He arched his eyebrows, and Poppy saw the doctor's face turn even more green, if that was even possible.

"I-I-I probably shouldn't have done that," he admitted as

he hung his head in shame. "I guess I panicked. She was having a kind of mental breakdown, and it seemed like a good idea to have her admitted. Though in hindsight, that was wrong of me."

"We talked to Clarissa," said Poppy. "And she didn't strike me as a person suffering mental problems at all. She has suffered a burnout, but that doesn't mean she's crazy."

"Her sister accused you of trying to get custody of Tommy," said Holt. "With his mother in a mental hospital, you would have no problem convincing a judge that the boy should live with you. Was that part of the rationale behind your actions?"

The doctor nodded slowly, not looking up to meet their eyes. He clearly was mortified that they had cottoned on to his evil little scheme. The ironic thing was that if he hadn't been abducted, the way he had treated his wife would probably never have come to light.

"Like I said, I panicked. When she first mentioned a divorce, I could already see the writing on the wall. She would get custody of Tommy and I would only see him once every two weeks if I was lucky. I love that boy to bits, and I just couldn't bear to be away from him for so long. And so I did something really stupid."

"And something really bad," said Poppy. "To lock Tommy's mother up in a mental hospital just so you could get custody of your son. That's a terrible thing to do, Doctor McMinn."

"I know," he said ruefully. "I see that now." He looked up, and Poppy saw that he had tears in his eyes and was wringing his hands. "I'll get her out of there as soon as possible. And whatever she wants to do, and whatever the judge decides, I won't contest it. Even if it means I won't see my son again."

Poppy cut her dad a look, and he rolled his eyes. So she

leaned forward and placed a hand on his. "I'm sure that it won't come to that. But I do think you should have a good long talk with your wife. Maybe you can still salvage your marriage? Have you tried couples therapy? It sure beats having your wife locked up in the loonie bin."

He nodded. "Thank you, inspector. For getting me out of the hands of that monster. And thank you for your kind words. I will talk to Clarissa. Maybe we can work things out."

As they walked him out, Poppy wondered how a clever man like Sandy McMinn resorted to such drastic and ill-advised measures to keep seeing his son. Even though in a sense she could understand the motivation behind his actions, he should have known that locking up the boy's mother would eventually lead to disaster, and when the boy was old enough and he found out what his dad had done, he might lose his respect anyway.

"The things people do for love," she said.

"You take a much too kind-hearted approach, honey," said Holt. "The way I see it, the guy should be punished for what he put his wife through at the hands of his 'good friend.' Though in all honesty, even I don't want to arrest him at this juncture."

"Please don't arrest him. It will only make matters worse. I think he learned his lesson."

"Let's hope so," said Holt, who didn't believe in the good-ness of people as much as she did. Considering how she had messed up with Bernard, maybe he was right.

CHAPTER 34

*T*he Atlas didn't look his Sunday best. What with the huge bruise on the side of his face, and the cut to his forehead, he looked more like a man who'd been through the wars than anything else. But then he probably shouldn't have tried to resist arrest when a pair of burly POSA team members were adamant about capturing him. They didn't fool around and had probably seen the resistance The Atlas put up as a challenge.

"I'm going to press charges, you know," he said as he gingerly touched his lip, which sported a nasty cut. "Police violence. You had no right to treat me like that."

"You do know that there was a warrant out for your arrest, right?" said Holt, who didn't feel one iota of compassion for the brute seated across the table from him. "So legally we were obliged to take you into custody, whether you liked it or not."

"All I did was pay a visit to my doctor," said that man. "What's wrong with that? Can't a man visit with his doctor?"

"Oh, absolutely," said Holt, "but not when you abduct the

doctor first. Now what's all this about you wanting an operation? I mean, I look at you and that spot isn't so bad."

He wasn't messing with the guy. After all the stories he'd heard, he'd expected half the man's face to be one big spot, but as it was, it was a lot vaguer and subtler than he'd thought.

"I've had work done in the past," said the gangster as he carefully placed a hand on the spot. "Laser treatment. Only it's not gone away completely. And so when I heard that Doctor McMinn had developed a revolutionary new technique to get rid of this type of birthmark, I knew I had to go and see him. Only you guys were making it very hard for me to do that, and so I had no other choice but to take a different approach."

"Look, I don't care about that birthmark of yours one way or another, Ari," said Holt. "But you can't go around abducting people just for the heck of it."

"Oh, go to hell," the tall man growled as he directed a menacing look at Holt. His fingers were bunched into fists, and Holt saw the veins at the side of the man's neck stand out like cables. He had no doubt his prisoner was about to jump out of his chair and wrap those hands of his around his neck. "You don't know what it's like to go through life being ridiculed by every single person you meet. From the people staring at you on the street, to the kids teasing you in school. It's the story of my life." His face worked.

"Your sister didn't tease you, did she?" asked Poppy.

The man's expression softened. "No, she never did. She was probably the only one. Even my dad hated my guts. He was embarrassed that he had a son like me. Not my mom, though. She was fine with it, and Margo. But even they couldn't protect me. And so I had to find a way to protect myself. And I have."

"So why now? Why get rid of this birthmark now?" asked Holt.

"Because I'm sick and tired of the nonsense!" said The Atlas as he jumped up and pounded his fist on the table, making it jump.

"Settle down, Ari," said Holt.

"I stand out," growled the gangster. "And that's never a good thing."

"Rumor has it that you're thinking about pulling a disappearing act?" asked Holt. "And that you need this stain to be removed so you can leave the country without attracting attention?"

"That's part of it," said the man as he took a seat again. "I've made my fortune, so now it's time to retire. Only I can't do that with a face like this," he said as he pointed to the port-wine stain. "And so I need to get rid of it once and for all." He settled back, folding his arms across his chest. "And now let's talk about Margo. Have you found her killer yet?"

"No, we haven't," Holt admitted.

"But we are following several promising lines of inquiry," said Poppy.

The gangster grinned, displaying two rows of perfect teeth. Probably courtesy of his sister's services. "That's what you cops always say when you have absolutely no clue what's going on. So let me tell you what happened. Bayton killed her. He wanted to get to me, and the only way he knew how was to kill my sister and hope that would draw me out."

Holt was shaking his head before the guy was finished talking. "Out of the question," he said. "Much as I often disagree with Commissioner Bayton, I know he would never do something like that. No, someone else killed Margo, Ari."

The guy frowned. "Of course you would defend that pig." He tapped the table with his index finger. "But he did it. I'm sure of it. He was hoping I'd show my face at Margo's funeral and then he could arrest me. Only now I probably won't even be allowed to go to her funeral."

"I'm sure something can be arranged," said Holt.

"What about Margo's boyfriend?" asked Poppy.

"Who?"

"Orvo Cross."

"That fitness teacher? No way. He's too chicken. He knows that if I find out he's behind this, I'll wring his puny little neck. And besides, why would he kill Margo? She was going to marry the guy."

Holt shook his head. "Margo may have wanted to marry Mr. Cross, but he didn't want to marry her."

The Atlas stared at him, his expression darkening. "He didn't want to marry my sister?"

"No, he didn't. For him this was just a meaningless fling, and he didn't have any intention of marrying Margo."

For a moment, the man was speechless, then he suddenly castigated the table again with his meaty fist, making it dance, and screamed, "I'll get that moron! I'll rip his head off and piss into his skull, the disrespectful—"

"Easy now, Ari," said Holt, holding out his hands.

But it was obvious that the man was too upset for the interview to continue. And so he and Poppy quickly left the room, while a couple of officers entered to make sure The Atlas didn't tear the entire room apart.

"You don't think he did it, do you?" asked Poppy as they watched through the one-way mirror as The Atlas raged and fumed. "I mean, he could have killed his sister."

"But what's the motive?" asked Holt.

"No idea. But he certainly is capable."

Before the cops could stop him, The Atlas roared and picked up the table and hurled it at the one-way mirror.

Then he picked up a chair and started battering it against the wall.

The man certainly had a lot of pent-up anger.

But had he used it to murder his own sister?

Holt didn't think so. But he could be wrong.

CHAPTER 35

*B*efore he returned home that night, Holt paid his usual visit to his parents to pick up Harley. When Mom saw her son arrive with Poppy in tow, she seemed confused.

"But I thought you had moved in with that boy? Bernie? Bertrand?" When Holt grinned, she said, "Help me out here, Glen. I know it starts with a B and it's French. Barney?"

"Bernard, Grandma," said Poppy. "But we…" She glanced over to her dad.

"Poppy and Bernard split up," he said, coming to his daughter's aid. "Just one of those things, you know."

They had agreed not to mention to Poppy's grandparents that Bernard was actually a serial rapist. Though more than likely, Holt's dad would find out sooner or later. As the former commissioner of their local police force, he still kept in touch with his old colleagues, and especially Ezekiel, the current commissioner, who was an old friend of his.

"Oh, that's too bad!" said Mom, who hated people splitting up. She was an avid reader of the gossip magazines, and whenever celebrities split up, she invariably expressed the fervent hope they wouldn't be able to live without each other and would get back together again when they came to their senses. And when inevitably they moved on and had a different conquest within the week, she was always crushed. "You have to work out your differences, honey," she said as she patted Poppy's hand. "Marriage is not a noun, you know. It's a verb. It takes a lot of work to make it work, just ask your grandad and me."

"So much work," Holt's dad said as he pulled a comical face.

"Oh, you," said Mom as she lightly slapped his arm. She turned back to her granddaughter, a look of concern on her face. "Whatever he did, I'm sure you can work it out."

"I doubt it, Grandma," said Poppy.

"Whatever it is, I'm sure he didn't mean it."

Poppy merely smiled, which gave her grandmother hope.

"See? I knew you'd see things my way. Work at it, honey. What does your father say?"

"Well..." said Poppy, giving her dad another look.

"I say she has to figure this out for herself," Holt said.

"Well, there you go," said Mom. "You should introduce him to the rest of the family. I'm sure we would all like to get to know this nice young man of yours. Wouldn't we, Mitch?"

Holt's dad looked up. "Mh? Oh, absolutely. I can't wait to meet Bertrand."

"Bernard!" Mom said. She gave Poppy a smile. "Right?"

"Right," said Poppy as she picked up Harley and decided to take him into the backyard. Holt got the impression she wasn't too keen on more of her grandmother's love advice.

"So what's going on with Auntie Lori?" he asked, also eager to change the subject. "I heard she got her money back?"

"She did!" said Mom. "All of it. Although at first the bank was being difficult, as usual. They said it was her fault for losing her money, and they couldn't do anything. It took a lot of phone calls and even a personal visit to the bank manager from Mitch to make them see the error of their ways. But in the end, it turned out that they could retrieve the money, and so it's all back now."

"I warned her about phishing," said Dad. "But does she listen? No, instead she lets this clown into her home and hands him her bank card and her PIN!" He shook his head. "You can try to protect people all you want, but you can't protect them from their own stupidity."

"But he said he worked for the police!" Mom argued. "And he was wearing a police uniform."

"So? These people will do anything to get their hands on your money. They will lie and they will cheat. That doesn't mean you have to make it easy for them by doing as they say."

"But she thought he was a cop!" said Mom. "And our generation has been taught always to do what the police tell you to do. It's drilled into us from when we are small."

"And that's exactly what these people are banking on," said Dad. "They target the older generation, raised to respect and trust authority figures and always follow instructions."

"It's a pest," Holt agreed. "Good thing we managed to catch them and get Auntie Lori's money back for her."

"So how is work?" asked Dad.

"Oh, you know," said Holt as he took a seat at the kitchen table. "We just managed to save a plastic surgeon who had been abducted by a gangster who wanted to have his appearance surgically altered and figured this was the best way to go about it."

"He wanted to have his appearance changed?" asked Mom, immediately intrigued.

"He has this big wine-port stain," said Holt, gesturing to the side of his face. "He wanted to get rid of it, but he was wanted by the police, so he couldn't walk into a clinic without possibly being arrested, so he figured he'd abduct the plastic surgeon instead."

"Oh, I think I saw that on the news," said Dad. "Famous gangster, right? And his sister was murdered—she was a dentist. Bad business, that."

"A murdered dentist?" asked Mom, looking shocked. She pressed a hand to her chest. "Who would murder a *dentist*? We *need* dentists. There aren't enough of them. Did you know that Brien Goodman has also stopped taking on new patients? It's a real problem. No dentist in this village is taking on new patients. If you're unlucky and you haven't already secured a dentist, you'll have to travel to the next town to find one."

"That's too bad," said Holt as his dad shot him a grin. How they had gone from the abduction of a plastic surgeon to the shortage of dentists was beyond him, but then Mom often had a logic that was entirely her own.

"Of course if we hadn't lost Eloy Stalls, this wouldn't have happened," said Mom. "That botched operation—we're still suffering the consequences to this day. He was struck off, you know. And so now we're one dentist short." She shuffled off and disappeared into the backyard, eager to have another chat with Poppy and offer her some more boyfriend advice.

"Struck off?" asked Holt.

"It's a crazy story," said Dad. "This guy claims Stalls damaged a nerve when he pulled a wisdom tooth, and now half his face is paralyzed, so he decided to take Stalls to court for pain and suffering. And the crazy thing is the judge sided with the guy and now we're one dentist short. I believe he was your Aunt Gardenia's dentist. She says he was just great."

"That's too bad," said Holt. "I didn't even know about that." But then he hadn't gone to the dentist in far too long. The rule was that you went once a year at least, but what with the divorce and his transfer to Loveringem, he'd had other things on his mind this past year.

Poppy came hurrying into the house, Harley on her trail. She shot Holt a pleading look. "Can we go now, Dad?"

Clearly she had had enough of her grandmother's advice already and was ready to leave. And so he got up and gave his dad a hug. "See you, Dad."

"See you, son," said his dad warmly. "And be careful out there," he added with a wink.

At least Dad got the joke.

CHAPTER 36

*I*t was the first night in a while that Poppy slept 'at home' again. Technically, it was still her name on the lease, but since she had more or less moved in with Bernard, she hadn't slept there for quite a while.

"It's good to have you home," Holt said, and meant it, too. He hadn't thought it was possible, but he had missed his daughter. He'd even missed her crappy cooking. Even though she was a lousy cook, they still had arranged to share the burden of preparing dinner. He didn't mind that half the time she cooked pasta. He loved pasta, and he had to admit that she was getting better at it. She didn't even burn the pasta sauce these days, or let the pasta boil to a soggy mess.

"Yeah, I missed it too," she admitted.

She looked a little sad, he thought, which had to be expected. After all, she had just found out that her boyfriend was a rapist and had probably assaulted over a dozen women. Plus, he was a drug addict and also a dealer.

"Next time I'm doing a background check on every single one of my boyfriends," she said, showing that she was thinking the exact same thing he was thinking. "And if I happen to forget, I'm giving you permission right now to do the same, Dad."

"Let's hope it won't be necessary." He'd much prefer not to have to investigate Poppy's boyfriends. Then again, after this latest experience, it was understandable how she wanted to make sure that next time there were no hidden criminal records to contend with.

"I mean, if companies ask for a clean record when they hire a person, why not us, right? Maybe Tinder should include it in their setup: you can only create an account if you prove that you don't have a criminal past."

"Even ex-cons deserve to have a dating life, honey," he pointed out. "And not all ex-convicts relapse. A fair few of them change their ways after a stretch in the pokey."

"I doubt that," she said darkly. Clearly, she wasn't in an optimistic frame of mind.

"Why don't I cook dinner?" he suggested. "And make us something special?"

"Yeah, I'm not really in the mood to cook," she admitted. "Imagine what would have happened if Georgina and the others hadn't caught Bernard? I might have ended up marrying a rapist. Or even having kids together. Imagine him being caught ten years from now. How could he do something like that? How could he..." Her voice broke, and she burst into tears. He hugged her, and she buried her face into his chest, sobbing uncontrollably and letting it all out while he held her.

He felt a familiar anger bubble up inside him. Anger at a no-good punk who had taken advantage of his daughter and might have ended up killing her if he'd gotten the chance.

And as she expressed her grief and upset at the betrayal and shock of discovering that Bernard was a criminal, he gently rubbed her back. Things could have been a lot worse. He could have lost his daughter today. The sobering thought made him wonder what he could have done differently. What he *should* have done differently and would do in the future.

To be honest, he didn't think there was a lot he could do. Even though he could look into the background of Poppy's boyfriends, it was a slippery slope. The next kid could be above suspicion in every way, but if he found out that his father-in-law had been digging into his past, he might not be as eager to pursue the relationship.

Then again, he had the impression that it might be a while before Poppy set foot on the dating path again.

After two disappointments in a row, she might put her love life in the freezer for now.

He just hoped she wouldn't be off men in general. He wanted her to find a good husband and start a family at some point. Even though he didn't think he and Leah had always set the right example, they still had done their best not to let their personal differences affect the way they raised their two kids.

Poppy sniffled and blew her nose in a napkin. "Okay, so this is the last time I'm shedding any tears over that rotten guy. He doesn't deserve my tears. He just doesn't."

"It's all right, darling," he said. "You will need time to grieve."

"And can you please tell Grandma that I'm never getting back together with Bernard? She seems to think that I shouldn't give up on him quite so soon."

"She doesn't know what kind of person he is. If she knew, she wouldn't act like this."

"Maybe we should tell her? Otherwise she'll just keep on pestering me, and I don't think I can stand much more of this."

"Yeah, maybe I'll tell her," he said. "When the time is right."

He disappeared into the kitchen to whip up a nice meal,

and as he did, he found his thoughts flashing back to the conversation at his parents' place. Harley came sniffing at his feet, and he threw him a piece of sausage. The dog barked, producing his usual happy sound, and he stared at him. Between Harley barking and his parents' stories, something clicked. "Well, I'll be..." he muttered as he fed the French bulldog another piece of sausage.

Was it possible? It almost seemed too outrageous a thought to contemplate. But then again, wasn't that often the case?

CHAPTER 37

Georgina was glad that The Atlas was behind bars, but even more than that, she was relieved that her attacker had been identified and wouldn't be able to hurt more women. The only part of the arrest that prevented her from being fully satisfied with the outcome was that her attacker had proven to be Poppy's boyfriend. Talk about a shocker for the ages!

She just couldn't imagine how Poppy would feel right now, with Bernard having been placed under arrest and accused of attacking over a dozen different women.

It was hard to imagine living under the same roof with the guy and sharing his bed. It was enough to make you feel sick.

And the worst part was that Poppy seemed to feel guilty, even though she had done absolutely nothing wrong. She had even apologized to Georgina on Bernard's account. Which was totally outrageous, and Georgina had told her as much.

"I mean, it isn't Poppy's fault that her boyfriend turned out to be a psychopath," she said now as she poured more fizzy water into her glass. She and her two housemates were in the living room of the house they shared, enjoying a meal. It wasn't a sumptuous one, as they had simply ordered Indian takeaway, but she loved it anyway. She was a sucker for Indian food, and Rasheed always knew what to get—probably because his aunt and uncle owned the restaurant they habitually ordered from. "My heart broke when she gave me that guilty look, you know. As if she was to blame for what he did."

"That's crazy," said Leland as he munched down on a chapati. They were dwindling fast, but then they didn't have any right to taste so good. "I mean, Poppy shouldn't have to apologize for what Bernard did. *He* should apologize to *her*."

Georgina's absolute favorite was palak paneer—spinach curry with fresh cheese, which she just couldn't get enough of. And aloo gobi, of course—crisp golden potatoes and cauliflower. Though to be absolutely honest, everything tasted delicious, and she couldn't believe it had taken her so long to discover this amazingly tasty cuisine.

"I feel sorry for Poppy," said Rasheed. "She looked so sad. And to imagine he actually attacked her. She could have died."

"I can't believe she didn't take time off work," said Leland. "If I had gone through what she had, I'd take a month off to lick my wounds. Maybe longer."

"She's tough," said Georgina. "But then I guess she takes after her dad in that respect."

Just then, there was a tap at the door, and they all looked up. "Are we expecting a visitor?" asked Leland.

Rasheed shook his head. "Not me." He got up to open the door, and while he did, Georgina took the opportunity to load more kofta onto her plate—Indian meatballs made of minced lamb, onions, and spices.

"God, this is so good," she said. "Who needs pizza when you can eat this stuff?"

"Yeah, it's pretty tasty," Leland agreed. "So do you think that The Atlas is the one who killed his sister? I mean, if he is, we will have closed three cases in one day. That has to be some kind of record, right?"

Georgina talked around her food. "Holt doesn't seem to believe so. He said The Atlas vehemently denied being behind his sister's murder, and he said he believes him."

"I don't know," said Leland. "I mean, the guy is a vicious, ruthless gangster, and we've seen that he's capable of extreme violence. He practically rearranged our entire interview room, and it took six cops to settle him down and escort him back into his cell."

"Motive, Leland," Georgina pointed out. "By all accounts, The Atlas adored his little sister. Why would he kill her? And besides, he thinks that Terrence is responsible. He even had that brick thrown through the commissioner's window."

"Yeah, I guess," said Leland reluctantly. He so wanted to clear their caseload that he was willing to cut corners and accuse the wrong person—which was a big no-no in anyone's book, but certainly in their chief inspector's.

She craned her neck to look into the hallway and see what was taking Rasheed so long. And then she saw it: it was Rasheed's mom who was making a beeline for the kitchen, even as Rasheed was trying to waylay her.

"Uh-oh," she said in a low voice. "Incoming!"

And then the woman was upon them. And for some reason looked extremely unhappy—with her!

She came to a full stop in front of Georgina and stood there glowering at her, arms folded across her chest, eyes shooting sheets of flame in her direction. "I thought my son asked you to move out?"

"What?" she said. Of all the things she had thought this woman was about to say, this was the last thing she expected.

"Don't act like you're innocent," said the woman. "I told Rasheed to get rid of you."

"But why?" she asked.

"Because it's improper for a young man like my son to live under the same roof as an unmarried woman, that's why. All of my friends are talking about it, and also all of my family. And it's all because of you!"

"Mom," Rasheed said in a pleading tone. "I told you that there's nothing going on between me and Georgina."

"That's absolutely inconsequential," said the woman, who was formidable, Georgina had to admit. Like a matron of old, she was tall and big and would probably take a crane to dislodge from the position she occupied in front of Georgina. Any moment now, she would probably start shifting her from the scene bodily—kicking her out of the house.

But unfortunately for her, she had picked the wrong target. Filled to the brim with delicious food, Georgina was feeling pretty good, and she wasn't about to let some hysterical harridan with weird notions about impropriety dislodge her from her home.

"Excuse me," she said as she got up and went toe-to-toe with the woman. "But this is my home, and you have absolutely no right to tell me whether I have the right to be here or not. And now I would like you to leave, please."

"If there's anyone who is leaving, it's you," said the woman as she tapped Georgina's chest with a finger.

Rasheed groaned, and Leland snickered.

"Oh, no, you didn't," said Georgina, gritting her teeth. And so she grabbed the woman's finger and twisted it.

"Hey!" said Rasheed's mom. "That hurts!"

"I hope it does," said Georgina. "And now you're going to apologize for the things you said about me."

"I'm not apologizing," said the woman as she tried in vain to extricate her finger from the other woman's grip.

"You'd better, or else I'm going to make you."

"You're the one who should be apologizing, for ruining my son's reputation."

"If there's anyone ruining Rasheed's reputation, it's you."

"I'm his mother! I only have his best interests at heart!"

"You could have fooled me. Now tell me you're sorry."

"I'm not! You're the one who should be sorry!"

It looked as if they had reached some kind of impasse, with neither of the two women willing to budge. Which is when a small voice piped up, and Rasheed's face materialized in Georgina's field of vision.

"Can you please let go of my mom's finger, Georgina?" he asked politely. "And can you please stop treating my friend and colleague like a common criminal, Mom?"

"If I'm treating her like a criminal, it's because she has done something really bad, and until she realizes this and clears out of the house, I won't stop," said his mom.

The gauntlet had been thrown down, and since Georgina was always up for a challenge, she figured she might as well go the full hog. And so she twisted the woman's arm until she was on the floor, with Georgina's knee pressing down between her shoulder blades.

"Oh, dear," Rasheed muttered as he closed his eyes.

"This will teach you not to tell me to move out of my own home," she said between gritted teeth. "Or to call me names."

"You're hurting me, you stupid girl!" said the woman.

"And still she persists," said Georgina. "Unbelievable."

Rasheed was wringing his hands helplessly. "Can you please let go of my mom?" he asked. "She has arthritis, and this is definitely not good for her."

"Rasheed, hit this woman over the head!" said the woman. "Do it now, before she kills me."

"I'm not going to hit Georgina over the head, Mom," said Rasheed.

"Then you're dead to me," she said from her impossible position on the floor. Even though she was at a disadvantage, she wasn't giving up, which was definitely something Georgina could appreciate. The woman had grit!

And so she decided not to torture her any longer. Rasheed was right. She wasn't a young person, and this wasn't helping anyone. Possibly, she had allowed herself to get carried away.

The moment she let go, Rasheed helped his mother to her feet. The woman had lost none of her anger, for when she regarded Georgina, it was with such hatred in her eyes that the latter felt the impact in her gut.

"If you're not out of this house by this time tomorrow, I will return and kick you out personally," she warned.

"You and whose army?" said Georgina.

"Oh, I'll bring my army," said the woman as she dusted herself off. "Just you wait and see. And now," she told Rasheed, "you will come with me. You will not stay here one moment longer, living in sin and being a disgrace to your family."

"I'm not coming," said Rasheed. "This is my home now, and these are my friends and my colleagues."

For a moment, Georgina thought she would strike her son, but in the end, she must have understood that this was a bad idea. Instead, she turned on her heel and stormed off. The door slammed, and then she was gone.

"Phew," said Georgina. "What was that all about?"

"She's certainly something else," said Leland, who hadn't moved from his position at the table and had probably eaten half the food while no one was looking.

Rasheed hung his head. "I'm in so much trouble now," he said.

Georgina gave him a pat on the back. "She'll come around," she said. "She has to."

"No, she won't," said Rasheed. "You don't know my mom. When she gets an idea into her head, nobody can talk her out of it. She's very stubborn that way. She believes that me living here with you is a bad thing, and she won't change her mind."

She felt for the guy, but if his mother thought that she was going to move out just because she had some funny ideas about men and women living under the same roof, she had another thing coming. And besides, where was she going to go? This arrangement suited the three of them perfectly.

"She'll change her mind," she said, taking a seat at the table again. "She has to—if she doesn't, she has a screw loose."

Judging from Rasheed's face, she had just described his mother to a T.

"It's just that she's very traditional," he said as he joined them. "She lives for tradition. And also, she's very worried about her reputation and what other people think of her and her family. If people know that I'm living here with an unmarried woman, they'll start to say bad things about me and consequently my family. And they'll shun my mother. And in her mind, that's just about the worst thing that can happen."

"People would do that?" asked Georgina.

"Oh, absolutely. And it will crush her—and possibly drive some of her patients away. For sure it will destroy my family's restaurant as people will start to boycott the place."

All in all, it certainly was a dilemma that Rasheed was being faced with—him and the rest of them, as they were in this together. And as they tucked into their meal again, she wondered if there wasn't anything they could do to fix this.

CHAPTER 38

Holt was still thinking about his brainwave from the night before when Roy Hesketh dropped by the station and took a seat at his desk.

"You look entirely too pleased with yourself," Holt said. "What gives?"

"Well… remember how Terrence took over that investigation of the canal barge murder?"

"I remember it all too well," he said dryly.

"Guess where The Atlas had been staying while he disappeared?"

He frowned, but his curiosity was piqued. "Go on, where?"

"The barge next to our unfortunate victim, Barney Waller. We did a perimeter search, like we always do, and talked to all of the neighbors. The barge moored next to Barney's had been occupied by The Atlas for the past couple of months. Not that anyone ever saw him, but when we knocked on the door, we found the boat empty, even though there were plenty of signs someone had been staying there and left in quite a hurry. DNA samples were taken, and they were a match for The Atlas. And now we come to the big question."

"What made The Atlas clear out in such a hurry?"

"Exactly. We think he's the one who killed Waller. So, with your permission, I would like to interrogate The Atlas and see if we can't get him to fess up to the man's murder."

"Be my guest," said Holt. "Though I have to warn you: he hasn't been a model prisoner so far. Pretty much demolished one of our interview rooms—though some would argue that he made some improvements, as it was a disgrace to begin with."

"So I probably should have a couple of uniforms in there while I talk to the guy?"

"That would be my suggestion. At least if you want to keep your face looking the way it does now. He is an extremely violent man."

"Yeah, I can tell from what he did to Waller," said Roy as he got up. "Pretty messed-up character, if you ask me, this Atlas fellow."

"He's got great teeth, though," said Holt. "No doubt courtesy of his sister." He also got up. "Want me to join you?"

"Nah, I think I can handle it," said Roy. But to be on the safe side, Holt decided to watch and make sure that The Atlas didn't reconstruct his friend's face.

Even with two officers present, standing next to The Atlas, and the prisoner handcuffed to the chair, Roy still kept a safe distance, just in case the man pulled a Samson on him and managed to break his shackles.

"So I wanted to ask you about your neighbor," said Roy as he placed a picture of Barney Waller in front of the criminal.

"Never seen him before in my life," The Atlas grunted after he cut a quick look at the picture.

"He was living next to you for months," Roy explained. "Occupied the barge moored next to yours."

The Atlas grinned, and once again Holt found himself admiring the man's perfect teeth. He wished his were as white and even as his, and wondered what his secret was for keeping them in such great shape. Brushing three times a day maybe? Or some secret toothpaste?

"I've never set foot on a barge, old man. I get seasick on boats."

"And yet we have found plenty of evidence that you were the person living on this barge," said Roy, placing more pictures in front of the guy. "We even found one of your favorite sweaters tucked underneath the mattress."

"That's not mine," The Atlas grunted.

"So why was your DNA on it? And why were your fingerprints all over the barge and its contents?"

The Atlas displayed those perfect rows of teeth again. He seemed to be in a pretty good mood today. Hopefully, they'd be able to limit the damage to their infrastructure this time. "You tell me, clever guy."

"Look, we can play games all day," said Roy, "but the judge will accept this as irrefutable evidence that you were Waller's neighbor for the past couple of months. Until the day he was murdered and you suddenly decided it was in your best interest to stop being his neighbor. Now, I wonder why that was. Did he happen to recognize you one night? And you were afraid he'd rat you out to us?"

The man's grin faded. "The Atlas is never afraid. Not of you or anyone else."

"And yet you decided to get rid of this guy by beating and knifing him to death." He placed more pictures on the table. "Pretty viciously, I might add."

"Nothing to do with me," said The Atlas.

"So you won't mind if we scrape those fingernails of yours and see if we can't find some of Mr. Waller's DNA? You may think to yourself: but I washed my hands. I scrubbed them. But I'm here to tell you that even if you did, there's every chance that some of Mr. Waller's DNA will still be found there. A minuscule amount is enough for a conviction. Or your clothes," he added, gesturing to the man. "Or your hair. Or any part of your anatomy, really. As I understand, you weren't expecting to be arrested when my colleagues picked you up at that clinic, so you may not have had time to get rid of all of your clothes—your shoes…"

"You cops," The Atlas spat. "With your obsession with digging into a person's body cavities. You're nothing but a bunch of sick perverts. Always going on and on about searching intimate areas of a person's body. And you love it, don't you? You love it!"

"Look, we can do this the easy way or the hard way," said Roy as he started gathering the images on the table. "But either way, we are going to get you for the murder of Mr. Waller."

The Atlas thought for a moment, then finally growled, "It was an accident, all right? All I wanted was to have a little chat. You know, to explain that I was his friend. But instead of treating me like a normal neighbor paying him a friendly, neighborly visit, he acted all jumpy and tried to call the cops. I hate it when people don't show me the respect that I deserve. So I grabbed his phone and threw it against the wall. And when he picked up a knife, I took that from him as well." He sighed and shook his head. "And then for some reason that I still don't understand, he decided to impale himself on the knife."

"He impaled himself on his own knife," said Roy, not hiding his skepticism.

"He did. I figured he was one of those irrational people who do these strange and unthinkable things. Self-harmers, you know. Basically, he committed suicide in front of me. And since I didn't want to get involved, I left." He lifted his shoulders, causing the handcuffs to rattle. "I know I should have called an ambulance, but it was obvious that the man was dead. And also, it was a traumatic experience for me, and I felt distraught. I wanted to be alone with my thoughts so I could process everything I had seen."

"Right," said Roy. "That's why the man was stabbed sixteen times, and his head was practically severed from his body. Because he decided to commit suicide in front of you."

"Hey, what can I tell you? Maybe he was depressed." That grin was back. "One of those sad, senseless deaths, huh?"

Roy seemed to be having trouble containing his anger, but in the end, he decided not to be goaded by this maniac. So instead, he left the interview room and joined Holt.

"The guy is a monster," he said, not mincing words.

"Yeah, he is. But a monster with very nice teeth."

"That's true," said Roy.

"So do you think you have enough on him?"

"Yeah, we'll build a nice case against the guy. He's not getting out for a very long time."

"Looks like he'll have to keep being The Atlas for a little while longer," Holt determined.

CHAPTER 39

*H*olt decided to put in a call to Sandy McMinn. He found the man in a mood of contrition. "Yeah, I'm moving out," he told him. "First thing I did this morning was go to pick up Clarissa from that clinic, and then I told her I was moving out of the house if that's what she wanted. I also apologized unreservedly for what I did to her. Even though she was suffering from a breakdown, that was no reason for me to have her committed."

"So you're getting a divorce?" asked Holt.

"Well, I asked her if she wanted a divorce, and she said yes, and I'm going to respect her wish. I was still hoping maybe we could fix things, but after the stunt I pulled, that's unlikely to happen. And so I've contacted a moving company, and I will move my stuff out of the house."

"Do you have a place to stay?" asked Holt, who was sympathetic to the guy, in spite of the suffering he had caused his wife. He knew that divorces can make people go a little crazy, and he actually felt sorry for the surgeon.

"Yeah, I'll stay with my brother for the time being. And I'll put my stuff in storage until I figure out what to do next." He sighed deeply. "I have to say that between the divorce and the kidnapping, it feels as if my life has slowly spiraled out of control. Then again, except for the kidnapping, I know I only have myself to blame for the mess that I'm in right now."

"It will work itself out," he said.

"You speak from experience, chief inspector?"

"I do, yeah. I mean, nothing as drastic as having my ex-wife locked up in a mental hospital, mind you. But I also had my moments when I lost the plot and did some crazy stuff." And even though he probably shouldn't, he ended up telling the guy what he'd done when he discovered that Leah was having an affair.

"Wow, that's... yeah, that is crazy," said the surgeon. "The thing is that my wife isn't having an affair, and neither am I. So I don't really know what caused our marriage to break down like this. I would love to ask her, but now is not the time."

"You probably should have asked her before you had her committed," he suggested.

"Yes, I know," he said ruefully. "That was not one of my best moments. I guess I panicked when I thought of her taking Tommy away from me."

"Will you get a chance to keep seeing your son?"

"Yeah, for now we've worked out some kind of arrangement."

"Good," he said. "That's good." He had been in the fortunate situation where both his kids were grown up, so he didn't have to go through this joint custody thing, which was hard for everyone. "Listen, there's something I wanted to ask you, doctor. A medical question."

"Of course. Is this in connection with my abduction?"

"No, this is connected to a different case altogether."

* * *

When Poppy walked into the office, she found her dad staring out in front of him, his fingers steepled and his brow furrowed. She took a seat in front of him, and he woke up as if from a reverie.

"Oh, honey, you didn't have to come in today."

"I wanted to," she said. "The worst thing right now would be for me to sit at home and think about what happened. I want to keep working, Dad," she said adamantly. "So don't send me home, please."

"If you feel you're up to it," he said.

"I do," she confirmed, nodding. "I really do. So what's with the look?" she asked, gesturing in his general direction.

"Mh? Oh, I think I just had an idea."

"I figured as much. You always get this look when you've had a breakthrough."

"Well, I wouldn't necessarily call it a breakthrough," he said. "It's just an idea. Quite possibly it's just a load of nonsense. But I still would like to take it for a spin."

"Okay, what's the idea?"

When he told her, she had to admit it sounded a little far-fetched. But then again, it wasn't beyond the realm of possibility either, so there was that to be said for it. "And now you want to test it—how?"

"Well, first I'd have to talk to Shonna," he said, referring to the prosecutor. "And if she agrees the idea has merit, she would have to apply for a warrant. And if the examining magistrate agrees, then we're in business—possibly."

"A lot of ifs," she said. She got up. "Okay, so let's go."

"Go where?" he asked, giving her a look of surprise.

"Well, the prosecutor's office, of course. No time like the present."

He grinned. "You know, I was worried about you. Figured I'd have to miss you for a couple of months while you recovered from your ordeal. But looks like you're powering through."

"Of course I'm powering through. That bastard isn't going to get the better of me." But as she and her dad walked out of the office, she had to admit that it had taken her the better part of the morning to convince herself that it was a good idea to get out of bed, get dressed, and drive to work. Dad had been very careful not to wake her up that morning, and had clearly expected her to stay home for at least the next couple of days or weeks.

But then she had decided she wasn't going to let this man ruin her life and her career. She wouldn't give him the satisfaction. The day before, Commissioner Simpson had told her that she could take time off for as long as she wanted to, and he had also set up a first chat with the police shrink.

She would take him up on the offer of the shrink, but not of the time off. Like she had told her dad, she couldn't imagine sitting at home in her PJ's while she chewed on the events of the day before. Going over every single detail of her relationship with Bernard, from the moment they met to the moment he had tried to drug her and do who knows what else to her. It had certainly been one of the more impactful events of her life, but she couldn't let him win. She just couldn't.

And so she was glad to be in the thick of things—just until she trusted herself enough to figure out where things had gone so terribly wrong. And how she could have allowed herself to be fooled by that horrible man.

* * *

SHONNA TURNER STUDIED Holt for a moment before turning pensive. "You're right. It is a long shot."

He and Poppy were in the prosecutor's office, located in

the Palace of Justice in the north of Ghent. He hoped she'd give the all-clear on his cockamamie idea. If not, he had no idea how else to prove what he felt in his gut was a possible solution to the case.

"If my dad says there's a high likelihood this is what happened," said Poppy, "then this is what happened. You know as well as I do that he's never wrong."

The corners of Shonna's mouth quirked up into a rare smile. As usual, she had her dark hair pulled back from her high forehead and was dressed in one of her dark power suits. Like Holt, she was good at what she did, even though you would never be able to accuse her of following her instincts the way he did. "I wouldn't go that far, Poppy," she said. "I can remember a few clunkers where your dad was pretty wide of the mark." She studied her fingernails for a moment—perfectly manicured, Holt couldn't help but notice. "But you're right. He's more right than wrong, and his track record is exemplary. Too bad he sometimes allows his famous gut feeling to cloud his judgment." She cut him a scrutinizing look. "How are things between you and Commissioner Bayton now?"

"Fine," he assured her. "We've worked things out and left all of that animosity behind us."

"Is it true that Leah is pregnant?"

She had slipped that one in, taking him by surprise. He moved uncomfortably in his chair. "Um, yes, I believe so."

"Well, good luck to her," said Shonna. "I never saw the great attraction of having kids."

"You... don't have kids?" asked Poppy.

"No, I don't," Shonna said. "And fortunately for me, my ex-partner and I were on the same page in that regard. When one partner wants kids and the other one doesn't, it has a tendency to make things very difficult."

Holt couldn't imagine not wanting to have kids, even

though it had taken some convincing on Leah's part for him to agree to trying for a baby. At first, he had argued that they should probably wait until he was a little further on his career path, but Leah said it was non-negotiable, and she'd been pregnant two weeks after they had that conversation. Even back then, she had been the person who wore the pants at home. Something that Terrence was only starting to discover now.

"Okay, so I'm going to talk to Judge Blackthorn, and if she agrees, you can start the operation. But Holt?" She gave him a warning look. "If word leaks about this, and it turns out you were wrong? Heads will roll, and it won't be mine, understood?"

"Understood."

"Good. Just so we're on the same page."

CHAPTER 40

*S*ebastian nursed his hot cup of coffee. Premium brand, of course. He'd been poor for most of his life, until he met and married Margo, whose parents had been pretty well off. She had believed in him and convinced her parents and her brother to invest in his dream of owning and operating a nightclub in their hometown of Ghent. Through sheer luck and grit, it had worked out, and soon he'd been the owner of several clubs, which had turned his life around and made him a very wealthy man.

The best thing that happened to him, though, was when Ruby had walked back into his life. He had known her way back when, when he was dabbling in producing records for some of the local acts. Not that he knew a lot about being a producer, or even less about launching and operating a record label, but that hadn't stopped him from giving it a shot.

The only artist that had survived those crazy years was Ruby. In fact, she was probably one of the country's most successful artists now, and in no small part owed it to that first record deal that she had signed with Sebastian's label.

She'd gone from strength to strength, and eventually had become too big for Sebastian and had moved on to one of the major labels, who had taken her career into the stratosphere, for local standards at least.

So when they had met backstage a couple of months ago, during a gala where Ruby was being given some award, he had discovered that the years hadn't diminished the affection he had always felt for her. And much to his surprise, the feeling had been mutual.

She had confessed that she still thought about him often, and that she sometimes wished they had stayed together. But then her success had made that impossible, and even though he had hated that they had drifted apart, he had understood.

She had to follow her dream, and he wasn't part of it.

Now, though, they were both in a position to give their relationship a second chance. Especially since she was the one who needed him, not the other way around. Even though she had a team dedicated to her career, there were certain things she couldn't share with them.

She took a seat in the breakfast nook and watched as he poured her a cup of coffee.

"Are you sure this is all right for you?" he asked.

She nodded, and said, in that hoarse voice of hers, "It's not exactly beneficial, but it can't do any harm either. At least that's what the doctors told me."

"Warm beverages are supposed to be good for the voice," he said. At least that's what he had always heard. "Though they probably mean tea, not coffee or hot chocolate."

She smiled. "I like how concerned you are about me, Seb."

"Of course I am concerned about you," he said as he started buttering a piece of toast for her. One big change was that these days Ruby was very health-conscious, and would be extremely careful about what she put into her mouth. Back then she had been a big fan of junk food, but that was out of the question now. And he understood, of course. No alcohol, either, which was detrimental to a singer's voice, just like cigarettes.

"Has that police detective been in touch?" asked Ruby.

"Haven't heard from him in a couple of days," Sebastian said. "Last time we spoke, he said that he had a solid lead."

"What lead would that be?" asked Ruby with a frown of concern drawing a groove between her perfect brows.

"He seems to think that Margo's brother had something to do with her murder."

"Oh, he's that criminal, isn't he?"

"Yeah. They call him The Atlas, on account of this big mark in the shape of an atlas he has on his cheek. They arrested him last week for the murder of a man who lived on a barge, and also the kidnapping of a plastic surgeon. He wanted him to make that mark disappear."

"And so he kidnapped him? I like his style."

"He's a hardened gangster, that's for sure."

This past week had brought him plenty of surprises, not least of which was the arrest of one of his bartenders who had been accused of spiking the drinks of several of his customers and also rape. It certainly had plummeted the reputation of the Marquee, one of his most profitable and popular clubs, where several of the victims had been attacked by the man. And also the Star, where Bernard had worked. So much so he'd had to close them both down for the time being. There would be a full rebrand, and the clubs would reopen under a new name and new management—even though he'd still be the owner, of course.

The idiot was going to cost him a lot of money. Too bad he hadn't been more vigilant in keeping an eye on the guy. Or reacted to the complaints when they started surfacing. That kind of thing often led to an avalanche of complaints that could bring a business to its knees, as had happened to several of his competitors. And now it had happened to him.

"So they think that this Atlas killed Margo?" asked Ruby.

"That was the impression I got," he confirmed. "Though these cops never really tell you anything, do they? Not until the case goes to court. And even then you often have to wait until the lawyers have their say. I guess they have to play their cards close to their vests, otherwise if word gets out what they really think, the bad guys might take advantage."

Ruby giggled. "Are you calling yourself a bad guy?"

"I guess I am," he quipped.

She coughed, and he gave her a look of concern. "How is the voice?"

"The same. Always the same." She tried to sing a few bars of one of her greatest hits, and instead of the velvety tones that she was famous for, she sounded like a croaky frog.

God, how he felt for her. What a waste.

"You know, I don't regret a single thing," she said as she traced her finger around the rim of her cup. She looked up. "Do you?"

"No, I don't regret a single thing either," he said. And he meant it. To have gone through what Ruby had gone through was absolutely tragic. And it was all Margo's fault—no question. He still couldn't understand how she could have made such a big mistake. She had always been so careful and so professional.

"I'm glad," Ruby said as she trailed a finger along his hand. Shivers ran up his spine and he got goosebumps. Even now, after all those years, he was still crazy about her. That feeling had never gone away. He had loved Margo, of course, but that passion, that insane attraction, had only struck him once.

"So many lost years," he said as he studied her.

"We can make up for them now," she said as she walked

around the kitchen counter and wrapped her arms around him. For a moment they shared a deep kiss. She tasted like coffee, and he supposed he did, too.

"Let's never be apart again," she suggested when they finally broke the kiss. "From now on, let's always be together."

"But what about your career?"

"What career? If my voice doesn't come back I won't have a career anymore."

"And you're okay with that?"

She shrugged. "Not really. But what choice do I have? I've seen all the specialists, both here and abroad, and they all say the same thing: there's nothing they can do." She traced a long fingernail along his cheek. "I need to hear you say it, sweetheart."

"What?"

"Do you love me?"

"You know I do."

"Say the words."

"I love you, Ruby."

"Even though I lost my voice?"

"Even though you lost your voice."

Her gaze intensified.

"And... do you forgive me?"

He smiled. "Yes, I do."

"Say it, darling. I need to hear it."

"I forgive you for murdering my wife."

CHAPTER 41

*I*t was as if all hell broke loose. The front door burst open and a small army of cops suddenly erupted onto the scene, screaming and yelling something Ruby couldn't understand. They were dressed like riot cops in full battle gear, as if she and Seb were a couple of heavily armed gangsters or highly dangerous terrorists or something. Once they had ascertained they weren't armed, they were forced to lie on the floor, which was extremely humiliating, since she was only dressed in her nightie and a housecoat. The next thing she knew, they were both handcuffed behind their backs and dragged to their feet.

"What's going on!" she yelled.

The cops dispersed and started going through Seb's apartment, throwing books off the shelves and ripping up the pillows on the couch. What were they looking for?

Then a burly man strode in, dressed in a long black overcoat and looking as if he may have been a professional wrestler in a previous life. She recognized him as Chief Inspector Holt. He was followed by a smallish woman with a pixie face wearing plastic gloves. It was his daughter Polly or Poppy or something. Behind her were a stocky woman, an Indian man, and a guy with a face like a ferret. They swarmed out across the apartment and joined in the search.

Only the big man and the pixie woman joined her and Seb. The armed police, or whatever they were, had placed them on a pair of chairs, and Ruby demanded, "What the hell do you think you're doing?"

Unlike her, Seb managed to keep his cool, for he simply said, "Good morning, chief inspector. Mind telling us what's going on?"

"What's going on is that you're both under arrest for the murder of your wife, Sebastian. Ruby for the actual murder and you for covering up a crime."

"You must be mistaken," said Seb. "I wasn't even here when Margo was killed, remember?"

"No, but you were, weren't you, Ruby?" said the big man as he turned to her. "In fact, you stabbed her to death right here in this apartment, didn't you? Later that night, Sebastian helped you get rid of the body by dumping it into the canal, cleaned up the mess, got rid of the knife, and made sure you could never be linked to the crime."

"Though you probably shouldn't have been spending time at his apartment when we dropped by," said Holt's daughter. "If you hadn't, you would have never been on our radar."

She'd known that was a mistake. Seb had even told her. But how were they to know that this inspector would drop by? She could have stayed in the bedroom while they were talking to Seb, of course. But she hadn't thought they'd suspect her. Wasn't finding a killer all about motive?

"Tell us where the knife is, Sebastian," demanded the chief inspector. But Seb decided to keep shtum.

Ruby stuck out her chin. "Why would I do such a truly terrible thing? I didn't even know the woman."

"Oh, yes, you did," said Holt. "She was your dentist. And mostly she did a good job. Until she didn't."

She stared up at the man, trying to maintain a defiant pose, but thinking back to that awful day, she couldn't manage. Tears sprung to her eyes as she remembered. She still didn't know what exactly had gone wrong. It could have been the anesthesia, or maybe when Margo worked on her tooth, she hit a nerve. All she knew was that after that fateful day, her voice had never recovered.

"Look, you don't have to keep up the pretense," said Holt. "See this?" He held up a smallish electronic device. "It's a bug. We've put them all around the apartment. We've been listening to your private conversations all week, and they've revealed a lot of interesting information. So we know everything, Ruby. We know you blamed Margo for destroying your voice and consequently your career. And we know you killed her and that you asked your lover Sebastian to help you cover it up and make sure that we wouldn't suspect you."

Holt's daughter dabbed at Ruby's eyes with a tissue paper to wipe away the tears, and that's when she lost it and finally broke down. "You've heard everything?" she breathed.

"Everything," Holt confirmed.

"You had no right to do that, Holt," said Seb.

"Oh, yes, we did," said Holt, and produced a piece of paper. "This is a warrant for the search of your apartment, a warrant for your arrest, and one for a surveillance operation targeting you and Ruby. So any information we gleaned will be accessible in court and will prove beyond a shadow of a doubt that you both conspired to kill Margo."

"I hated her so much," said Ruby, hanging her head. "She destroyed me. My career meant everything to me. My voice —it's my instrument. My life. And she took that away from me. And the worst part is that she didn't even admit that she made a mistake. She said it was just a coincidence that I lost my voice after she worked on my tooth. But I know that it was her. I've seen the best doctors in the world, and they all said the same thing: irreparable damage to my vocal cords as a consequence of a botched dental procedure."

"Margo was a brilliant dentist, but she must have had an off day," said Seb quietly. "Or maybe she wasn't paying attention. Whatever it was, she ended up destroying Ruby's life."

"If only she had apologized," said Ruby. "And tried to work with me to come up with a solution. But every time I talked to her, she insisted that she wasn't to blame and that I was making a mountain out of a molehill."

"She was afraid for her professional reputation," said Seb. "That she would be struck off."

"I didn't want to file a complaint against her," said Ruby. "I didn't want to ruin her life, too. But in the end, I knew I had to. And that's when she started threatening me. Said she knew people who would deal with me and it wouldn't be pretty. Asked if I was attached to the way I looked and if I wouldn't mind if my face got cut up so bad no one would recognize me anymore and I'd have to live in a hole from now on—hiding from the world."

"I told Ruby that Margo's brother was some kind of crime kingpin, so her threats were all too real."

"She was going to ask her brother to 'deal with me,'" said Ruby. "To cut me up and make sure I'd never talk again."

"And that's when I came up with the idea to silence Margo," said Seb. "Ruby and I had recently gotten reacquainted after many years, and the old flame still burned just as bright as it always had. And I was afraid that Margo would never agree to a divorce. If I filed for divorce, I'd have to contend with Ari, and I'd be the one to be cut up into little pieces."

"Don't say that it was your idea, Seb," she said warmly. "You know it isn't true."

Now it was Seb's fault to break down into tears. "It *was* all my idea!" he said.

"No, it wasn't. And Chief Inspector Holt knows this. He's been listening to us."

"How did you end up asking Margo to work on your tooth, Ruby?" asked Holt.

"That was my fault," said Seb. He looked up at the chief inspector. "Ruby and I met at some gala show in Antwerp a couple of months ago. I saw she was suffering from a severe toothache. So I told her to pay a visit to Margo. That she would fix her tooth in no time."

"You weren't to know, Seb," she said. "And I don't blame you. Though I have to say that I have often wondered if perhaps Margo knew that we had been lovers and that she secretly tried to take revenge by messing up my voice. But the doctors I talked to said that it was extremely unlikely that she had done it on purpose. They said most likely it was a fluke."

"She had been drinking a little the night of the gala," said Seb. "So maybe her hands weren't as steady as usual? Or her coordination was off?"

They had talked about this over and over—incessantly, in fact. And she had asked the doctors all these questions. The truth was that no one could have predicted this outcome.

"If only she hadn't threatened to have her brother cut me up if I didn't drop my accusations," said Ruby. "That's when I knew I had to get rid of her. That it was either her or me." She gave the chief inspector a look of defiance. "And you know what? I don't regret it, Mr. Holt. I'm glad I killed Margo. She was a horrible person and I'm glad she's dead."

"Better get dressed, Ruby," said Holt's daughter as she removed the handcuffs.

Oddly enough, there was a softness in her tone and a

kindness in her gaze as she escorted her up the stairs to the bedroom to put on some clothes.

And then she remembered that the woman had proclaimed she used to be a big fan when she was a kid.

Too bad she and Seb hadn't been more careful.

Looked like they wouldn't be together after all.

CHAPTER 42

*F*urther interrogation revealed that Sebastian hadn't been aware of Ruby's plans to kill Margo. It was even possible that she hadn't been aware herself. According to the singer, she had dropped by the house to give Margo one last chance to own up to her mistake and try to make things right. The dentist had become nasty, in Ruby's words, and had threatened to tell her brother to get rid of Ruby once and for all. Things got heated and finally the fight had turned physical, with Ruby grabbing a carving knife from the knife block in the kitchen and stabbing Margo in the throat with it. She had bled out right in front of her.

When Sebastian finally arrived home, there was nothing he could do for Margo, who was dead on the floor in a pool of blood. And so he had taken things in hand and together he and Ruby had carried Margo's body out to the canal and rolled her in. Then they had smeared some of Margo's blood on the grass and Ruby had uttered a blood-curdling scream, hoping that people would think that Margo had been killed while out for a jog.

The whole thing had taken maybe ten minutes, but Ruby's heart had been racing throughout, afraid they'd be caught. Lucky for them, the coast had been clear, and they had hurried back to the apartment to clean up the mess. Unbeknownst to them, both Barney Waller and The Atlas had heard the splash, and had looked out of the portholes of their respective canal barges. When The Atlas saw the look of recognition on Barney's face, that had sealed the latter's fate. Even Sebastian hadn't known that his notorious brother-in-law was living not more than a hundred meters from the apartment. Only Margo had known.

Back at the apartment, Sebastian had put the knife in the dishwasher, removing all traces of the crime, and they had hoped that the police wouldn't finger them as potential suspects.

The only mistake they had made was for Ruby to stay at the apartment. She should have left that night and not contacted Sebastian for weeks, until the hubbub had died down. By sticking around, and even moving in with her lover, she had painted a big red target on her back that Holt couldn't miss. When Poppy led the singer upstairs to go and change, she asked her in tremulous tones how long she would have to go to prison for, and Poppy had explained that it all depended on the judge and the jury—if the case ever went to trial.

"Get a good lawyer," she advised the woman. "They'll help you navigate the process."

Even though Ruby had committed a terrible crime, she still couldn't help but feel for the singer. She had lost her voice and that had clearly driven her to the edge of her sanity.

"Mainly it was my mom who put the idea into my head," Holt explained now.

He and Poppy had invited the rest of the team to the

house, and Holt had cooked for them. And even though Georgina, Leland, and Rasheed were mostly aware of how everything had gone down, Holt still managed to surprise them with a few details they had been in the dark about. Like the fact that Holt had found inspiration in his mother's stories.

"She told me about a person whose face had become paralyzed after a visit to the dentist. And then I remembered that Ruby seemed to have some kind of trouble with her voice. And so I put two and two together and wondered if there could possibly be something in that."

"And lo and behold," said Georgina, "there was!"

She seemed in fine fettle, Poppy thought, and had recovered well from her ordeal at the hands of Bernard. The same couldn't be said about her. She still woke up in the middle of the night and expected her ex-boyfriend to stand over her, wielding that syringe and threatening to hurt her.

The shrink she had started seeing on the commissioner's instigation had told her it would be quite a while before she worked through what had happened to her. Even though she might feel fine now, she had taken a big hit, and a thing like that left its mark. She needed to be patient with herself, and treat herself with kindness.

Which is why she had decided to move back in with her dad. There was no one she felt as safe with as he. He'd never let anyone hurt her, and if only she had listened to him when she had first introduced Bernard to him, she wouldn't have found herself in this mess. His judgment was spot on.

Rasheed checked his watch. "I better get going," he said. "I promised my aunt I'd help out at the restaurant."

"Is your family still roping you into that?" asked Georgina. She didn't seem to agree with their colleague pulling an extra shift at the restaurant after hours.

"It's only temporary," he said. "They just had to let someone go, and they're a little short-staffed right now."

"They're taking advantage of you," said Georgina, who wasn't Rasheed's mom's biggest fan ever since she had a run-in with the woman at the house. She had told them all about it, and apparently it had been pretty epic.

"It's fine," said Rasheed as he pulled on his jacket. "See you guys tomorrow."

After he left, Georgina said, "His mom is trying to convince him to move back home. Just so he doesn't have to stay under the same roof as me. That woman is something else."

"It isn't easy for Rasheed," said Leland. "On the one hand, he wants to be his own man, and on the other, his family is putting a lot of pressure on him. I wouldn't want to be in his shoes right now."

"So someone should tell this woman what's what," said Georgina.

"Maybe that person shouldn't be you," said Leland. "After what happened last time, I think it's safe to say she hates you."

"Yeah, she is not my biggest fan. But then neither am I a big fan of hers. She treats Rasheed as if he's her personal slave or something."

"Who wants dessert?" asked Poppy, eager to show off the cake she had made. Even though her dad had made dinner—an excellent coq au vin—she had volunteered to try her hand at baking an actual chocolate cake. Truth be told, she'd had a little help from her grandmother, who was a master baker, but she had still done a lot of the work herself.

"I think I have some space left," said her dad as he gave her a wink. When she brought out the cake, she got a lot of oohs and aahs, and she was pleased as punch.

"Now that I've moved back in with you, Dad," she said, "I promise I'll try and pull my weight more in dinner prep."

And she meant what she said. She had even checked out cooking courses and had found that there was a cooking course at one of the many schools that Ghent boasted. She could finally learn how to cook. As she cut up the cake, she suddenly noticed that Rasheed had left his phone behind. She picked it up and ran out after him—hopefully, he hadn't left yet.

His car was just pulling away, and she waved the phone, hoping he would see her. He did and abruptly pulled to a stop and wound down the window. "Here you go," she said as she handed him the phone.

"I don't know where my head is at these days," he confessed. "Between my regular job at the precinct and my family pulling me in for extra shifts, my brain is getting all scrambly."

"Why don't you just tell your mom no?" she asked. "I mean, it can't be that hard to find an extra waiter. I'll bet there's plenty of people looking for a job."

"I know, but it's my mom, you know. And she's already worried about me, so..." He shrugged. "Just trying not to rock the boat, I guess. If it makes her happy to see me help out at the restaurant, I feel like she'll probably let me off the hook for living with Leland and Georgina at the house."

"Judging from what I heard, I doubt that very much," she said. "Seems to me she's trying to pull you more into the bosom of the family again, and trying to get you to move out of the house and in with them."

"I would never let that happen," he assured her. "Come hell or high water, I want to be my own person. I mean, don't get me wrong, I love my family. But they can be so..."

"Manipulative?" she suggested.

He grinned. "Something like that."

After he had driven off, she wondered if *she* shouldn't have a chat with Rasheed's mom. He wasn't merely her colleague, after all. He was also her friend. And as she walked back into the house, she promised herself that she would do just that.

CHAPTER 43

A week had passed since the stunning events that had transpired. Poppy was still not fully recovered from both Bernard's betrayal and the discovery that her childhood idol, Ruby Floss, was a killer. She found it hard to process both these events, but knew that over time she would get over it—especially Bernard.

She glanced in through the window of the Indian restaurant and wondered if she had picked the right one. Rasheed had given her the address when she asked him where it was —under the pretext that she also wanted to sample that delicious Indian food Georgina and Leland were always raving about.

She pushed in through the front door and found herself in a pleasantly decorated restaurant, with plenty of traditional Indian decorations adorning the walls. On the floor, a sumptuous red carpet sparked a deep sense of pity for the cleaners who had to keep it clean, but she had to admit it lent the place a lot of atmosphere.

She had only just walked in when a server already greeted

her, a big smile on his face. "The takeaway counter is over there," he said. "Or would you like a table, miss?"

"Yes, I would like a table," she said. "And is it possible to speak to a Mrs. Genner? I'm a friend of her son Rasheed." Even though Rasheed's mom was a dentist, just like her husband, the couple spent a lot of time at Rasheed's uncle and aunt's restaurant, which in fact was owned by the whole family, and so they all helped out as much as time allowed.

"Oh, absolutely," said the server. "I will tell her you asked to speak to her." He gave her a dazzling smile, and then led her to a booth in the corner.

She slid into the booth and picked up the menu that the server had handed her. She didn't recognize any of the names, but Georgina had given her a short list of menu items that she assured her she would adore, and so she checked it on her phone. She could have asked her dad along, but felt that it was probably better if she didn't. The mission she had assigned herself was a delicate one, and perhaps Holt wasn't the right person for the job. She wasn't even sure if she was.

A shadow fell over her, and she found a woman of sizable proportions studying her intently, a vague smile on her face. Her hands were folded, and she was dressed in traditional Indian garb. "You are a friend of Rasheed?" asked the woman.

"Yes, my name is Poppy," she said as she got up to shake the woman's hand. "And I work with your son."

"Oh," said the woman, her smile slipping off her face. "That means you're also a police officer?"

"That's correct."

The woman studied her for a moment but seemed intrigued enough to take a seat across from her. No hand-shakes were exchanged, though, which told Poppy that Rasheed's mom might have developed a dislike for all of her son's colleagues as a group.

"What did you want to talk to me about?" asked the

woman. She was polite enough but a little guarded, which wasn't hard to understand after the fracas that she and Georgina had engaged in. According to Leland, there had been screaming and even some low-level physical violence, two forces of nature colliding with no winners to come out of the face-off.

"The thing is, Mrs. Genner, that Rasheed finds himself in a very difficult situation. On the one hand, he loves his family very much. But on the other, he also loves his job and his colleagues. So he finds himself caught between a rock and a hard place at the moment. And it's starting to affect his work. Which, I think you will agree, is not an ideal situation."

"And you are telling me this why, exactly?" asked the woman as she brushed a lock of hair from her brow.

"Well, Rasheed told me that you object to the fact that he lives in the same house as two of his colleagues and that you would prefer it if he moved back in with his family."

"That is not what I said," said the woman determinedly. "Either Rasheed has been misrepresenting the facts, or you are deliberately distorting them and putting words in my mouth."

Poppy saw that she'd have to tread carefully if she didn't want to get kicked out of the restaurant in the next five minutes. "Well, he told me that you don't want him living under the same roof as his colleague Georgina—because she is a woman?"

"That is not what I said," said the woman, shaking her head. "I told him that his reputation will suffer if he keeps on living under the same roof as an *unmarried* woman. I have nothing against your colleague Georgina, but the fact that she isn't married, and neither is my son, creates a big problem."

"Because... he might be tempted to start something with her, you mean?" asked Poppy, trying to understand.

The woman gave her a tight smile. "I know that my son could never be seduced by her. For one thing, she isn't his type. At all. Too..." She gestured with her hand. "Manly. Rasheed likes his women more refined and feminine."

Poppy decided that this was a part of the conversation she would never share with Georgina. She might be tempted to walk in here and give Rasheed's mother another piece of her mind. "So what is the problem, exactly?" she asked.

The woman sighed. "Look, from the moment Rasheed was a little boy, his father and I selected the perfect wife for him. She's the daughter of a very good friend of ours, who is also my husband and his brother's business partner in the restaurant. The girl is the same age as Rasheed, and they grew up together, so they know each other well. The problem," she stressed, as her dark eyes bored into Poppy's, "is that her father heard about Rasheed moving into *that* house with *that* woman, and is threatening to cancel the arrangement. To revoke his permission and to promise his daughter to a different man. And even worse, he's also threatening to pull out of the restaurant and demand that we buy him out. And since he owns a large part of the business, that means we'd have to come up with the money to do so—which will pose quite a challenge. So now do you see what the problem is, Miss..."

"Holt," she said. "Yes, I can definitely see that this is quite the dilemma for you and your family." And it was definitely something that Rasheed hadn't discussed with them. According to him, this was all about his mother being old-fashioned and not wanting her son to live in the same house as a woman she didn't approve of. But things were clearly a lot more complicated than that. "Look, why don't I have a chat with your son? And maybe we can find some kind of middle ground?"

"There is no middle ground," said the woman stiffly.

"There is only one thing that can be done, and that is for Rasheed to move out of that awful place. And to get married to Laila and move in with her. That's the only solution. And if he can't see that..." She lifted her hands. "Then he's not the man I thought he was. I raised him better than to bring shame and hardship to his own family. To humiliate us all, out of sheer stubbornness."

"I'll talk to him," she said, though she now wondered why she had decided to take on the role of negotiator. She had a feeling things were going to prove a lot harder than she had anticipated. Especially since she got the impression—and she might be wrong about this—that Rasheed didn't have feelings for Laila. Or else he would have mentioned her. Then again, he was a very private person, and possibly didn't want to burden them with his problems.

"You do that," said the woman. "You talk to him and tell him that he's proving himself to be a big disappointment to us all. His father, his uncle, his brothers, the whole family. We're all suffering greatly because of this situation." She got up and held out a hand. "It's very good of you to do this for us," she said, and for the first time since Poppy had made the woman's acquaintance, there was a flicker of warmth in her gaze.

She shook the woman's hand and watched her sail off in the direction of the kitchen. Moments later, the server materialized at her table, and she gave him her order. Looked like she'd have to have another little chat with Rasheed.

Though to be honest, she couldn't really see a way out of this that would be satisfying for all parties concerned. Somehow, something would have to give. Either Rasheed got married to this girl, or he would end up having to disappoint his family. Either way, she was just the go-between. Meaning that it wasn't her problem to solve. And she was sure glad that it wasn't, for she had no idea how Rasheed should handle it.

As she waited patiently for her order to be brought out, she noticed that the server had left a small envelope and placed it on her empty plate. Curious, she picked it up and saw that it contained a piece of paper with a note. Wondering if this was an Indian tradition, she unfolded the note. The moment she read the now all-too-familiar message, her stomach gave a sudden lurch.

'I haven't forgotten,' the note read.

Also located in the envelope was a copy of a newspaper article. It told the story of the Loveringem pensioners being targeted by the gang of fake police officers. One name had been highlighted: that of her great-aunt Lori.

A chill ran up her spine. Was it possible that the same person who'd been sending her dad messages all this time had somehow managed to target Auntie Lori?

She immediately called over the server. "Did you put this envelope on my plate?" she asked.

"Yes," he said. "Yes, I did. Why, is there a problem?"

"Where did it come from?"

"Someone gave it to me just now and asked me to deliver it to you. Said he was your boyfriend and this was a game you two played from time to time. He delivers messages to you and vice versa." His face fell. "This man... he wasn't your boyfriend?"

"What did he look like?"

"Um... he was a good-looking young man. Brown hair, blue eyes. Quite handsome." His face had reddened considerably. "He was very friendly, so I didn't see the harm in playing along." When he saw the expression on Poppy's face, he brought a hand to his mouth. "I'm so sorry, miss. I should never have said yes. Was it a terrible message?"

She understood that the server hadn't meant any harm.

"It's all right," she said as she forced a smile. "It's just that I wasn't expecting it, that's all."

"So…" he studied her face. "I didn't make a mistake?"

"No, you didn't," she assured him. "No mistake at all."

He seemed extremely relieved and then offered her free drinks on the house, which she assumed he'd have to pay out of his own pocket.

"No, that's fine," she said. Then she thought of something. "You wouldn't happen to have a CCTV camera outside, would you?"

"No, I'm afraid we don't," he said. "We have one inside, to keep an eye on the customers." Once again, he slung a hand to his mouth, and his face turned scarlet. "I should not have said that."

"It's okay," she said. Too bad about the cameras, though. She wondered who this young man could have been. He must have been following her to know she was going to this restaurant. As the server hurried off, possibly to tell the kitchen to speed up her order, she studied the message, then carefully put it back into the envelope. She didn't expect there to be any fingerprints, but you never knew. She'd hand it over to the lab to have it processed for prints and DNA.

She knew exactly who was behind this, of course.

Brian Parnham. The butcher of Gentbrugge.

Even from inside his jail cell, he continued to cause trouble for Holt—and now for his family as well.

CHAPTER 44

*H*olt studied the note. It certainly gave rise to grave concern. "And you're telling me that this guy must have been following you?" he asked.

Poppy nodded. "There's no other explanation. How else would he know that I was going to be at that restaurant at that moment? And he specifically asked the server to deliver the message to me. He even described me, so he knew I was in there and what I looked like."

"Christ," he said as he put down the note. "Parnham is getting more and more brazen."

"He must be in communication with this young man," said Poppy. "Unless we're dealing with a fan?"

Holt grimaced. "That's an odd way to describe him." But Poppy was right. "Let's just hope that he doesn't go from being a fan to being a copycat."

"What did Parnham do, exactly?"

"He murdered an entire family of six. Father, mother, three daughters, and a son-in-law who happened to be on the premises when he decided to launch his murder spree. I was the one who caught him and got him locked up, and he clearly isn't happy about it."

"We have to look into this, Dad. He isn't going to stop."

"No, you're right. We have to identify this young guy and find out what he's up to. Whether it's just idle threats or if he's planning to take things one step further."

His daughter looked distinctly uncomfortable, and she had every right to be. If this guy was a copycat, he wouldn't stick to trying to steal Aunt Lori's money. He'd become a murderer.

"I'll talk to the guy who got locked up for the Aunt Lori business," he promised. "If he selected Lori as a consequence of Parnham's intervention, we need to know."

"Oh, and there's one other thing, Dad," she said.

He put down the book he'd been reading. Even though Poppy had told him a million times that he should get himself a Kindle and start reading books the digital way, he was an old-fashioned guy and still preferred to read his books on paper. Though recently, he did get himself an iPad and had started reading comics on it. The clarity of the images was unparalleled. Though he still missed the feel and the mystery of the paper version.

"What is it?"

"I talked to Rasheed's mom, and she told me this story about a wife she has already selected for him. It's the daughter of a businessman who's a partner in the restaurant Rasheed's family runs. And if he doesn't marry her, he'll pull out of the deal and demand they buy him out, which they can't. So it looks like this whole living under the same roof as Georgina is more complicated than Rasheed has made it out to be."

"This really isn't any of our business, Poppy," he said. "We don't want to start interfering in our colleagues' personal lives. The same way they don't interfere in ours." Though it had to be said that after he and Leah had divorced, a lot of well-wishers had given him all kinds of advice on how to start dating again—advice that he'd blithely ignored.

"It's affecting his work, Dad," she argued.

She was seated on the edge of the armchair, and he could tell she was determined to see this thing with Rasheed through. It was an admirable sentiment, but he didn't see what they could do to solve things for their colleague.

"You're his boss," she said. "And if his personal life is affecting his work life, that's something you need to address. Right?"

"I guess," he said as he rubbed his eyes. As if they didn't have enough to contend with, now he had to deal with the intricate and messy details of his detective's love life? "Look, why don't I have a chat with Rasheed? See what he has to say. But if he tells me to back off, don't expect me to turn all Mr. Matchmaker on him, okay? I'm not a dating expert."

Poppy had turned pensive again. "Maybe we could arrange a meeting of all parties involved? That way—"

"No," he said determinedly. "Absolutely not."

"Or maybe we could get HR involved?"

"No! It has nothing to do with us, honey."

"And I say it does. Rasheed isn't just our colleague. He's also our friend, and we owe it to him to—"

"Look, he's old and wise enough to decide for himself what he wants to do. And as far as I can tell, he's already made that decision. Otherwise, he wouldn't have moved in with Georgina and Leland. So I will talk to him, but I won't organize a roundtable discussion of the poor boy's love life. He'd be absolutely horrified, I can tell you that right now."

Poppy grinned. "No, I guess that would be outside of your purview."

"Thank you!" he said, as he gestured in her direction.

She plopped down next to him and dragged Harley onto her lap. The dog rewarded her with a lick on her face.

"I can't imagine having my partner selected for me from the moment I'm born," she said. "What if I don't even like him?"

"Maybe I should have done that," said Holt. "Me and your mom, I mean. Pick a boy to marry you?"

She slapped his arm. "Dad!"

"I could still do it, you know."

She gave him a dirty look. "Try it and feel my wrath."

"Isn't that what they do on these reality shows? Let the computer play matchmaker?"

"And more often than not, they get it totally wrong," she said as she picked up the remote and switched on the TV. Looked like he wouldn't get back to reading his novel.

"I'll bet I could do it. There's no one who knows you better than I do. And with my insight into the male psychology, I could probably find you the perfect partner."

"Like I said, try it and be prepared to feel the pain."

She selected one of the thriller series that they both liked so much and started the first episode. He smiled as he studied her face. Even though Bernard had hurt her something bad, she seemed fine. Though he also knew his daughter could seem perfectly bubbly on the surface, but often hid a deeper reality that she didn't share with anyone—not even her dad.

If only he could look straight into her heart and deal with whatever it was that was bothering her. But that was a superpower he did not possess. All he could do was be there and be ready for her when she did decide to open up about what kept her up at night.

As far as he was concerned, that's what being a dad was

all about. He tickled Harley behind the ear, and the bulldog settled in between the pair of them and sighed happily.

THE END

Thanks for reading! If you want to know when a new Nic Saint book comes out, sign up for Nic's mailing list: nicsaint.com/news

ABOUT NIC

Nic has a background in political science and before being struck by the writing bug worked odd jobs around the world (including but not limited to massage therapist in Mexico, gardener in Italy, restaurant manager in India, and Berlitz teacher in Belgium).

When he's not writing he enjoys curling up with a good (comic) book, watching British crime dramas, French comedies or Nancy Meyers movies, sampling pastry (apple cake!), pasta and chocolate (preferably the dark variety), twisting himself into a pretzel doing morning yoga, going for a brisk walk, and spoiling his feline assistants Lily and Ricky.

He lives with his wife (and aforementioned cats) in a small village smack dab in the middle of absolutely nowhere and is probably writing his next book right now.

www.nicsaint.com

f X ⓞ ⒷⒷ ⓐ ⓖ

Printed in Dunstable, United Kingdom